Harry Harrison was born in Stamford, Connecticut in 1925 and lived in New York City until 1943, when he joined the United States Army. He was a machine-gun instructor during the war, but returned to his art studies after leaving the army. A career first as a commercial illustrator and later as art director and editor for various picture, news, and fiction magazines fitted him only for a lifetime residence in New York, so he changed it for the freelance writer's precarious existence and moved his family to Cuautla, Mexico. Since then he has lived in Kent, Camden, Italy, Denmark, Spain and Surrey; he has now returned to his native land, but he has not ceased to wander. He rationalizes this continual change of residence as essential research, when in reality it is an incurable case of wanderlust that enables him to indulge all his enthusiasms: travel, skiing, practising Esperanto, and making an annual pilgrimage to the Easter Congress of the British Science Fiction Association.

By the same author in Orbit

Harry Harrison

The Technicolor®
Time Machine

The author gratefully acknowledges the kind permission granted by Technicolor Corporation of America for the use of its trade name and registered trademark in the title of this book.

Futura Publications Limited
An Orbit Book

An Orbit Book

First published in Great Britain in 1968
by Faber and Faber Limited

First Orbit edition published in 1976
by Futura Publications Limited

ISBN 0 8600 7887 6

Printed in Great Britain by
Hazell Watson & Viney Ltd,
Aylesbury, Bucks

Futura Publications Limited
Warner Road, London SE5

"What am I doing here? How did I let myself be talked into this?" L.M. Greenspan groaned as dinner scraped at his ulcer.

"You are here, L.M., because you are a far-sighted, quick-thinking executive. Or to put it another way, you have to grasp at any straw handy, because if you don't do something fast Climactic Studios will sink without a trace." Barney Hendrickson puffed spasmodically at the cigarette he clutched between yellowed fingers and stared unseeingly at the canyon landscape that rushed soundlessly past the window of the Rolls-Royce. "Or to put it even another way, you are investing one hour of your time in the examination of a project that may mean Climactic's salvation."

L.M. gave all of his attention to the delicate project of lighting a smuggled Havana cigar: clipping the end with his gold pocket clipper, licking the truncated tip, waving the wooden match about until all the chemicals had burned away, then gently puffing the slender greenish form to life. The car slid over to the curb with the ponderous ease of a hydraulic ram and the chauffeur rushed around to open the door. L.M. stared out suspiciously without moving.

"A dump. What could there be in a dump like that that could possibly save the studio?"

Barney pushed unsuccessfully at the unmoving and solid form. "Don't prejudge, L.M. After all, who could have predicted that a poor kid from the East Side slums would one day be head of the largest film company in the world?"

"Are you getting personal?"

"Let's not get sidetracked," Barney insisted. "Let's first go inside and see what Hewett has to offer and make our preconceptions afterwards."

Reluctantly, L.M. allowed himself to be urged up the cracked flagstone walk to the front door of the run-down stucco house and Barney held him firmly by the arm while he rang the bell. He had to ring twice more before the door rattled open and a small man with a large bald head and thick-rimmed glasses peered out at them.

"Professor Hewett," Barney said, pushing L.M. forward, "This is the man I talked to you about, none other than the head of Climactic Studios himself, Mr. L.M. Greenspan."

"Yes, of course, come in . . ." The professor blinked fishily behind his round glasses and stood aside so they could enter.

Once the door was closed behind his back L.M. sighed and surrendered, allowing himself to be led down a flight of squeaking stairs into the basement. He halted abruptly when he caught sight of the banks of electrical equipment, the festooned wires and humming apparatus.

"What is this? It looks like an old set for *Frankenstein.*"

"Let the professor explain." Barney urged him forward.

"This is my life work," Hewett said, waving his hand roughly in the direction of the toilet.

"What kind of life work is *that?*"

"He means the machines and apparatus, he's just not pointing very well."

Professor Hewett did not hear them. He was busy making adjustments at a control board. A thin whining rose in pitch and sparks began to fall from a hulking mass of machinery.

"There!" he said, pointing dramatically—and with considerably more accuracy this time—at a metal platform set on thick insulators, "That is the heart of the vremeatron, where the displacement takes place. I will not attempt to explain the mathematics to you, you could not possibly understand them, or go into the complex details of the machine's construction. I feel that a demonstration of the vremeatron in operation will be wisest at this point." He bent and groped under a table and brought out a dusty beer bottle that he put on the metal platform.

"What is a vremeatron?" L.M. asked suspiciously.

6

"This is. I shall now demonstrate. I have placed a simple object in the field which I shall now activate. Watch closely."

Hewett threw a switch and electricity arced from the transformer in the corner, the mechanical howl turned to a scream while banks of tubes flashed brilliantly and the air filled with the smell of ozone.

The beer bottle flickered briefly and the roar of the apparatus died away.

"Did you see the displacement? Dramatic wasn't it?" The professor glowed with self-appreciation and pulled a length of paper marked with squiggles of ink out of a recording machine. "Here it is, on the record. That bottle traveled back seven microseconds in time then returned to the present. In spite of what my enemies say the machine is a success. My vremeatron—from *vreme,* the Serbo-Croatian for 'time,' in honor of my maternal grandmother, who was from Mali Lošinj—is a workable time machine."

L.M. sighed and turned to the stairs. "A nut," he said.

"Hear him out, L.M., the professor has some ideas. It is only because he has been turned down by all the foundations in his requests for funds that he will even consider working with us. All he needs is some finance to jazz his machine up."

"There's one born every minute. Let's go."

"Just listen to him," Barney pleaded. "Let him show you the one where he sends the beer bottle into the future. This is too impressive to ignore."

"There is a temporal barrier in any motion towards the future, I must explain that carefully. Displacement toward the future requires infinitely more energy than displacement into the past. However, the effect still operates—if you will watch the bottle closely."

Once again the miracle of electronic technology clashed with the forces of time and the air crackled with the discharge. The beer bottle flickered, ever so slightly.

"So long." L.M. started up the stairs. "And P.S., Barney, you're fired."

"You can't leave yet—you haven't given Hewett a chance to prove his point, or even to let me explain." Barney was angry, angry at himself, at the dying company that employed him, at the blindness of man, at the futility of man, at the fact he was overdrawn in the bank. He raced up behind L.M. and whipped the smoking Havana from his chops. "We'll have a real demonstration, something you can appreciate!"

"They cost two bucks apiece! Give it back—"

"You'll have it back, but watch this first." He hurled the beer bottle to the floor and put the cigar on the platform. "Which one of these gadgets is the power control?" he asked Hewett.

"This rheostat controls the input, but why? You cannot raise the temporal displacement level without burning out the equipment—*stop!*"

"You can buy new equipment, but if you don't convince L.M., you're on the rocks and you know it. Shoot for the moon!"

Barney held the protesting professor off with one hand while he spun the power to full on and slammed the operation switch shut. This time the results were far more spectacular. The scream rose to a banshee wail that hurt their ears, the tubes glowed with all the fires of hell, brighter and brighter, while static charges played over the metal frames; their hair stood straight up from their heads and gave off sparks.

"I'm electrocuted!" L.M. shouted as, with a last burst of energy, all the tubes glared and exploded and the lights went out.

"There—look there!" Barney shouted as he thumbed his Ronson to life and held the flame out. The metal platform was empty.

"You owe me two bucks."

"Look, gone! Two seconds at least, three . . . four . . . five . . . six . . ."

The cigar suddenly reappeared on the platform, still smoking, and L.M. grabbed it up and took a deep drag.

"All right, so it's a time machine, so I believe you. But what has this got to do with making films or keeping Climactic off the rocks?"

"Let me explain . . ."

There were six men in the office, grouped in a semicircle in front of L.M.'s desk.

"Lock the door and cut the phone wires," he ordered.

"It's three in the morning," Barney protested. "We can't be overheard."

"If the banks get wind of this I am ruined for life, and maybe longer. Cut the wires."

"Let me take care of it," Amory Blestead said, standing and taking an insulated screwdriver from his breast pocket—he was the head of Climactic Studios' technical department. "The mystery is at last solved. For a year now my boys have been repairing these cut wires on the average of twice a week." He worked quickly, taking the tops off the junction boxes and disconnecting the seven telephones, the intercom, the closed circuit television and the Muzak wire. L.M. Greenspan watched him closely and did not talk again until he had personally seen all ten wires dangling freely.

"Report," he said, stabbing his finger at Barney Hendrickson.

"Things are ready to roll at last, L.M. All of the essential machinery for the vremeatron has been built on the set for *The Creature's Son Marries the Thing's Daughter* and the expenses have been covered by the budget for this picture. In fact there was a bit of a saving there, the professor's machines cost less than the usual props—"

"Don't digress!"

"Right. Well, the last laboratory scenes for the monster picture were shot this afternoon, yesterday afternoon I mean, so we got some grips in later on overtime and cleaned all the machinery out. As soon as they were gone the rest of us here mounted it in the back of an army truck from the set of *The Pfc. from Brooklyn* and the Prof has hooked it up and tested everything. It's ready to go."

"I don't like the truck—it'll be missed."

"No, it won't, L.M., everything has been taken care of. It was government surplus in the first place and was going to be disposed of in the second. It was sold legally through our usual outlet and bought by Tex here, I told you—we're in the clear."

"Tex, Tex—who is he? Who are all these people?" L.M. complained, darting suspicious glances around the circle. "I thought I told you to keep this thing small, hold it down until we saw how it works, if the banks get wind . . ."

"This operation is as small as it could possibly be. There is myself and the Prof, whom you know, and Blestead, who is your own technical chief and has been with you for thirty years—"

"I know, I know—but what about those three?" He waved a finger at two dark and silent men dressed in Levis and leather jackets, and at a tall, nervous man with reddish blond hair. Barney introduced them.

"The two in the front are Tex Antonelli and Dallas Levy, they're stunt men . . ."

"*Stunt men!* What kind of a stunt you pulling bringing in two phony cowboys?"

"Will you kindly relax, L.M. We need help on this project, trustworthy men who can keep quiet and who know their way around in case of any trouble. Dallas was in the combat infantry, then on the rodeo circuit before he came here. Tex was thirteen years in the Marines and an instructor in unarmed combat."

"And the other guy?"

"That's Dr. Jens Lyn from U.C.L.A., a philologist." The tall man rose nervously and made a quick bow toward the desk. "He specializes in German languages or something like that, and is going to do our translating for us."

"Do you all realize the importance of this project now that you are members of the team?" L.M. asked.

"I'm getting paid my salary," Tex said, "and I keep my mouth shut." Dallas nodded in silent agreement.

"This is a wonderful opportunity," Lyn said rapidly, with a slight Danish accent. "I have taken my sabbatical, I would even accompany you even without the generous

10

honorarium as a technical adviser, we know so little of spoken Old Norse—"

"All right, all right," L.M. lifted his hand, satisfied for the moment. "Now what is the plan? Fill me in on the details."

"We have to make a trial run," Barney said. "See if the Prof's gadget really does work—"

"I assure you . . . !"

"And if it does work we set up a team, work out a script, then go out and shoot it on location. And what a location! All of history is open to us on wide screen! We can film it all, record it—"

"And save this studio from bankruptcy. No salary for extras, no sets to be built, no trouble with the unions . . ."

"Watch it!" Dallas said, scowling.

"Not *your* union, of course," L.M. apologized. "All of the crew from here will be employed at scale and above, with bonuses, I was just thinking of the savings at the other end. Go now, Barney, while I am still enthusiastic, and do not come back until you have good news for me."

Their footsteps echoed from the cement path between the giant sound stages and their shadows stretched first in back, then in front of them as they walked through the pools of light under the widely spaced lamps. In the stillness and loneliness of the deserted studios they had sudden thoughts about the magnitude of what they were attempting and they moved, unconsciously, closer together as they walked. There was a studio guard outside the building who saluted as they approached and his voice broke the morbid spell.

"Tight as a drum, sir, and no disturbances at all."

"Fine," Barney told him. "We'll probably be here the rest of the night, classified work, so see that no one gets near this area."

"I've already told the captain and he's passed the word to the boys."

Barney locked the door behind them and the lights flared from the rafters above. The warehouse was almost empty, except for a few dusty flats leaning against the back wall and an olive-drab truck with the white army star on its door and canvas turtleback.

11

"The batteries and accumulators are charged," Professor Hewett announced, clambering into the back of the truck and tapping on a number of dials. He unhooked the heavy cables that ran to the junction box in the wall and handed them out. "You may board, gentlemen, the experiment can begin any time now."

"Would you call it something else besides experiment?" Amory Blestead asked nervously, suddenly beginning to regret his involvement.

"I'm getting into the cab," Tex Antonelli said. "I'll feel more comfortable there. I drove a six-by like this all through the Marianas."

One by one they followed the professor into the rear of the truck and Dallas locked up the tailgate. The banks of electronic machinery and the gasoline-powered motor-generator filled most of the space and they had to sit on the boxes of equipment and supplies.

"I am ready," the professor announced. "Perhaps for the first trial we might take a look in on the year 1500 A.D.?"

"No." Barney was firm. "Set 1000 A.D. on your dials just as we decided and pull the switch."

"But the power expenditure would be less, the risk even . . ."

"Don't chicken out now, Professor. We want to get as far back as possible so that no one will be able to reognize the machinery as machinery and cause us any trouble. Plus the fact that the decision has been made to do a Viking picture, not a remake of *The Hunchback of Notre Dame.*"

"That would be in the sixteenth century," Jens Lyn said. "I would date the setting in medieval Paris rather earlier, about . . ."

"Geronimo!" Dallas growled. "If we're gonna go let's stop jawing and go. It spoils the troops if you horse around and waste time before going into combat."

"That is true, Mr. Levy," the professor said, his fingers moving over the controls. "1000 *anno domini* it is—and here we go!" He cursed and fumbled at the controls. "So many of the switches and dials are dummies that I get confused," he complained.

12

"We had to make the machines so they could be used in the horror film," Blestead said, talking too fast. There was a fine beading of sweat on his face. "The machines had to look realistic."

"So you make them unrealistic, bah!" Professor Hewett muttered angrily as he made some final adjustments and threw home a large multipoled switch.

The throbbing of the motor-generator changed as the sudden load came on, and a crackling discharge filled the air above the apparatus: sparks of cold fire played over all the exposed surfaces and they felt the hair on their heads rising straight up.

"Something's gone wrong!" Jens Lyn gasped.

"By no means," Professor Hewett said calmly, making a delicate adjustment. "Just a secondary phenomenon, a static discharge of no importance. The field is building up now, I think you can feel it."

They could feel something, a distinctly unpleasant sensation that gripped their bodies solidly, a growing awareness of tension.

"I feel like somebody stuck a big key in my belly button and was winding up my guts," Dallas said.

"I would not phrase it in exactly that manner," Lyn agreed, "but I share the symptoms."

"Locked on to automatic," the professor said pushing home a button and stepping away from the controls. "At the microsecond of maximum power the selenium rectifiers will trip automatically. You can monitor it here, on this dial. When it reaches zero . . ."

"Twelve," Barney said, peering at the instrument, then turning away.

"Nine," the professor read. "The charge is building up. Eight . . . seven . . . six . . ."

"Do we get combat pay for this?" Dallas asked, but no one as much as smiled.

"Five . . . four . . . three . . ."

The tension was physical, part of the machine, part of them. No one could move. They stared at the advancing red hand and the professor said:

"Two . . . one . . ."

They did not hear "zero" because for that fraction of

13

eternity even sound was suspended. Something happened to them, something undefinable and so far outside of the normal sensations of life that an instant later they could not remember what it had been or how it had felt. At that same moment the lights in the warehouse outside vanished, and the only illumination came from the dim glow of the instruments on the tiered panels. Behind the open end of the truck, where an instant before the brightly lit room had been, there was now only a formless, toneless gray nothing that hurt the eyes when you looked at it.

"Eureka!" the professor shouted.

"Anyone want a drink?" Dallas asked, producing a quart of rye from behind the crate he was sitting on, and accepting his own invitation to the marked detriment of the bottle's liquid contents. It passed quickly from hand to hand—even Tex reached in from the cab for a slug—and all of them, with the exception of the professor, drew courage from it. He was too busy at his instruments, babbling happily to himself.

"Yes—definitely—definitely displacing toward the past . . . an easily measured rate . . . now physical displacement as well . . . wouldn't do to end up in interstellar space or in the middle of the Pacific . . . oh dear no!" He glanced into a hooded screen and made more precise adjustments. "I suggest you hold securely to something, gentlemen. I have made as good an approximation as possible to the local ground level, but I am afraid to be too precise. I do not wish us to emerge underground, so there may be a drop of a few inches. . . . Are you ready?" He pulled the master switch open.

The back wheels hit first and an instant later the front of the truck jarred to the ground with a mighty crash, knocking them about. Bright sunlight flooded in through the open rear making them blink, and a fresh breeze brought the sound of distant breakers.

"Well I'll be double-god-damned!" Amory Blestead said.

The grayness was gone and in its place, framed by the canvas top of the truck like a giant picture window, was a view down a rocky beach to the ocean, where great waves were breaking. Gulls swooped low and screamed while

14

two frightened seals snorted and splashed off into the water.

"This is no part of California I know," Barney said.

"This is the Old World, not the New," Professor Hewett said proudly. "To be precise, the Orkney Islands, where there were many settlements of the northmen in the eleventh century, in the year 1003. It undoubtedly surprises you that the vremeatron is capable of physical as well as temporal displacement, but this is a factor—"

"Nothing has surprised me since Hoover was elected," Barney said, feeling more in control of himself and affairs now that they had actually arrived somewhere—or somewhen. "Let's get the operation moving. Dallas, roll up the front of the tarp so we can see where we're going."

With the front end of the canvas cover out of the way, a rocky beach was disclosed, a narrow strand between water and rounded cliffs. About a half mile away a headland jutted out and cut off any further view.

"Start her up," Barney called in through the rear of the cab, "and let's see what there is further along the beach."

"Right," Tex said, pulling the starter. The engine ground over and burst into life. He kicked it into gear and they rumbled slowly down the rocky shingle.

"You want this?" Dallas asked, holding out a holstered revolver on a gunbelt. Barney looked at it distastefully.

"Keep it. I'd probably shoot myself if I tried to play around with one of those things. Give the other one to Tex and hold onto the rifle yourself."

"Aren't we going to be armed just in case, for our own protection?" Amory Blestead asked. "I can handle a rifle."

"Not professionally, and we work to union rules around here. Your job is to help the professor, Amory. The vremeatron is the most important thing here. Tex and Dallas will take care of the armaments—that way we can be sure that there won't be any accidents."

"*Alt for Satan!* Look at that, so beautiful, that I should be seeing this with my own eyes!" Jens Lyn burbled and pointed ahead.

The truck had churned its way around the headland and a small bay opened up before them. A crude, blackened

15

rowboat was pulled up onto the shore, and just above the beach was a miserable-looking building made of clumsily piled turf and stone and covered with a seaweed-thatched roof. There was no one in sight, though smoke was curling up from the chimney hole at one end.

"Where is everybody?" Barney asked.

"It is understandable that the sight and sound of this truck has frightened them and that they have taken refuge in the house," Lyn said.

"Kill the engine, Tex. Maybe we should have brought some beads or something to trade with the natives?"

"I am afraid that these are not the kind of natives that you are thinking of . . ."

The rough door of the house crashed open as if to emphasize his words and a man leaped out, howling terribly and waving a broad-bladed ax over his head. He jumped into the air, clashed the ax against a large shield he carried on his left arm, then thundered down the slope toward them. As he approached them with immense bounds they could see the black, horned helmet on his head, and his flowing blond beard and wide moustache. Still roaring indistinctly he began to chew the edge of the shield: foam formed on his lips.

"You can see that he's obviously afraid, but a Viking hero cannot reveal his fear before the thralls and housecarls, who are undoubtedly watching from concealment in the building. So he works up a berserk rage—"

"Save the lecture, will you, Doc. Dallas, can you and Tex take this guy on, maybe slow him down before he breaks something?"

"Putting a bullet through him will slow him down a lot."

"No! Positively not. This studio does not indulge in murder, even for self-defense."

"All right, if that's the way you want it—but this goes under the personal jeopardy bonus in the contract."

"I know! I know! Now get out there before—"

Barney was interrupted by a thud, then a tinkling crash followed by even louder howls of victory.

"I can understand what he is saying!" Jens Lyn

16

chortled happily. "He is bragging that he has taken out the monster's eye . . ."

"The big slob has chopped off one of the headlights!" Dallas shouted. "Keep him busy, Tex, I'll be right with you. Draw him away from here."

Tex Antonelli slid out of the cab and ran down the beach away from the truck, where he was seen by the berserk axman, who instantly began to pursue him. At about fifty yards distance Tex stopped and picked up two fist-sized stones, well rounded by the sea, and bounced one of them in his palm like a baseball, waiting calmly until his raging attacker was closer. At five yards he let fly at the man's head and, as soon as the shield had been swung up to intercept the stone, he hurled the other at the Viking's middle. Both stones were in the air at the same time and even as the first one was bounding away from the shield the second caught the man in the pit of the stomach: he sat down with a loud woosh. Tex moved a few feet away and picked up two more stones.

"*Bleyoa!*"[1] the downed man gasped, shaking his ax.

"Yeah, and you're one too. C'mon buddy, the bigger they are, the harder they splat."

"Let's wrap him up," Dallas said, coming out from behind the truck and spinning a loop of rope around his head. "The Prof is getting jittery about his gadgets and wants to go back."

"Okay, I'll set him up for you."

Tex shouted some Marine Corps insults, but they did not penetrate the linguistic barrier. He then resorted to the Latin language of gesture that he had learned as a youth and with rapid movement of fingers and hands called the Viking a cuckold, a gelding, ascribed some filthy personal habits to him and ended up with the Ultimate Insult, left hand slapped to right bicep causing the right fist to be jerked up into the air. One—or more—of these obviously had antecedents that predated the eleventh century, because the Viking roared with rage and staggered to his feet. Tex calmly stood his ground, though he looked like a

[1] "Coward!"

17

pygmy before the charging giant. The ax swung up and Dallas's spinning lasso shot out and caught it, while at the same moment Tex put out his foot and tripped him. As the Viking hit the ground with a crash both men were on him, Tex paralyzing him with an armlock while Dallas hogtied him with rapid bights of rope. In a few instants he was helpless, with his arms tied to his legs behind his back and roaring with frustration as they dragged him through the pebbles back to the truck. Tex had the ax and Dallas the shield.

"I have to talk to him," Jens Lyn insisted. "It is a rare opportunity."

"We must leave instantly," the professor urged, making a delicate adjustment on the verniers.

"We're being attacked!" Amory Blestead squealed, pointing with palsied finger at the house. A ragged horde of shock-haired men armed with a variety of swords, spears and axes were rushing down the hill toward them.

"We're getting out of here," Barney ordered. "Throw that prehistoric lumberjack in the back and let's get going. You can have plenty of time to talk to him after we get back, Doc."

Tex jumped into the cab and grabbed up his revolver from the seat. He fired it out to sea until all the chambers were empty, raced the engine, flashed the remaining headlight and blew the horn. The shouts of the attackers turned to wails of fear as they dropped their weapons and fled back into the house. The truck made a U-turn and started back down the beach. When they came to the sharp curve around the headland a horn blasted from the other side of the rocks and Tex just had time to jerk the wheel to the right—until the tires were in the rush of breaking waves—as another olive-drab truck tore around the headland and roared by them.

"Sunday driver!" Tex shouted out the window and kicked the truck forward again.

Barney Hendrickson glanced up as the other truck went by, swinging into their wheel tracks, and was almost petrified as he looked into the open rear. He saw himself standing there, swaying as the truck lurched over the rocks and grinning wickedly. At the last moment, before the

18

second truck vanished from sight, the other Barney Hendrickson raised his thumb to his nose and wiggled his fingers at his duplicate. Barney dropped back onto a box as the rock wall intervened.

"Did you see that?" he gasped. "What happened?"

"Most interesting," Professor Hewett said, pressing the starter on the motor-generator. "Time is more plastic than I had ever imagined. It allows for the doubling of world lines, perhaps even for trebling, or even an infinite number of coils. The possibilities are incredible . . ."

"Will you stop babbling and tell me what I saw," Barney snapped, lowering the almost empty whiskey bottle.

"You saw yourself, or we saw us who will be—I'm afraid English grammar is not capable of accurately describing a situation like this. Perhaps it would be better to say you saw this same truck with yourself in it as it will be at a later date. That is simple enough to understand."

Barney groaned and emptied the bottle, then shouted with pain as the Viking managed to wriggle around on the floor and bite him in the leg.

"Better keep your feet up on the boxes," Dallas warned. "He's still frothing."

The truck slowed and Tex called back to them. "We're coming to the spot where we landed, I can see where the tire tracks begin just ahead. What's next?"

"Stop as close to the original position of arrival as you can. It makes the adjustments simpler. Prepare yourselves, gentlemen—we begin our return journey through time."

"*Tröll taki yor öll!*"[2] the Viking roared.

3

"What went wrong?" L.M. asked suspiciously as they trooped tiredly into his office, dropping into the same chairs they had left eighteen centuries before. "What happened—you walk out of the office ten minutes ago and

[2] "May the trolls take you all!" (A pre-Christian equivalent of "Damn you!")

now ten minutes later you walk in?"

"Ten minutes to you, L.M.," Barney said, "but it's been hours for us. The machine is okay, so we're over the first and biggest hurdle. We know now that Professor Hewett's vremeatron works even better than we had hoped. The way is open to take a company back in time and film an accurate, full-length, wide-screen, realistic, low-budget, high-quality historical. Our next problem is a simple one."

"A story."

"Right as always, L.M. And it so happens we have a story, a true-to-life story, and, what is more, a patriotic story. If I was to ask you who discovered America, what would you say?"

"Christopher Columbus, 1492."

"That's what most people think, but it was the Vikings who did the job first."

"Was Columbus a Viking—I thought he was Jewish?"

"Let us please drop Columbus. Five hundred years before Columbus was born Viking ships had sailed from Greenland and discovered what they called Vinland, which has since been proven to be part of North America. The first expedition was led by Eric the Red—"

"Kill that idea! You want to get us blacklisted with a commie picture?"

"Just hold on for a bit please, L.M. After Eric found the place it was colonized, Vikings came and lived there and built houses and farmed, and this was all organized by the legendary hero, Thorfinn Karlsefni . . ."

"These names! He's got to go too. I can already hear the big romance scene . . . kiss me my dearest Thorfinn Karlsefni she whispers. Out. You're not so hot, Barney."

"You can't rewrite history, L.M."

"What else have we ever done? This is no time to go soft on me, Barney Hendrickson, you who were at one time my best producer and director before the lousy moron-box ruined us all. Get a grip on yourself. The motion pictures are not primarily an educational medium. We are selling entertainment, and if it doesn't entertain it doesn't sell. I see it this way. We got this Viking, you call him Benny or Carlo or some other good Viking name, and you do a saga of his adventures . . ."

20

"That's just the word for it, L.M."

". . . like one day fighting, and winning of course, restless, he's that kind. He goes off and finds America then comes back and says I have found America! so they make him the king. Then there is this girl, with long, blond wig hair, who keeps waving to him every time he sails away and promises to return. Only now he is older with a little gray above the ears and some scars, he has suffered, and this time instead of going away he takes the girl with him and together they sail into the sunset to a new life as the first pioneers at Plymouth Rock. Well?"

"Great, as always, L.M. You haven't lost the touch." Barney sighed tiredly. Dr. Jens Lyn—whose eyes had been getting wider—made a strangling noise.

"B-but—it is not that way, it is in the records. Even Mr. Hendrickson is not completely correct. It was Leif Ericsson, the son of Eric the Red, who is generally credited with the discovery of Vinland. There are two versions of the chronicle, one in the *Hauksbók* and the other in the *Flateyjarbók*—"

"Enough!" L.M. grumbled. "You see what I mean, Barney? Even the history books can't agree, so with a little bringing together here and there and some touching up we got a story. Who were you thinking of for the leads?"

"If we can get him, Ruf Hawk would be perfect for the Viking. And someone who is really stacked for a girl."

"Slithey Tove. She's available and between pictures and for two weeks her crumb of an agent has been in and out of here with deals, so I know she is broke and we can get her cheap. Next you will need a writer, and for that use Charley Chang, we have him on contract. He's a specialist."

"On Bible stories, maybe, not historicals," Barney said doubtfully, "and frankly I didn't think much of *Down from the Cross* or the other thing, *Walking the Red Sea Waters*."

"Ruined by censorship, that's all. I okayed the scripts myself and they were great—" He broke off suddenly as a bellowing cry sounded through the wall. "Did you hear that?"

"It's the Viking," Tex said. "He was still aching for a

21

fight so we slugged him and chained him to the shower in the executives' head."

"What's this?" L.M. scowled.

"An informant," Barney told him. "One of the locals. He attacked the truck so we brought him along so that Dr. Lyn could talk to him."

"Get him in here. He's just the man we need, someone with local knowledge to answer some questions on production problems. You got to have a local who knows his way around when you are shooting on location."

Tex and Dallas went out and, after a few minutes of chain rattling and two loud thuds, returned with the slightly glassy-eyed Viking. He stopped in the door when he saw the men waiting in the room, and they had their first clear look at him.

He was big, even without the horned helmet he was almost seven feet tall, and hairy as a bear. Matted blond hair hung below his shoulders, and his flowing moustache vanished into the waves of beard that fell to his chest. His clothing consisted of coarsely woven blouse and breeks held in place by a varied assortment of thick leather straps, and they exuded a rich odor of fish, stale sweat and tar, yet the heavy gold bracelet around his arm did not seem out of place. His eyes were a light, almost transparent, blue, and glared at them from under beetling brows. He was battered and chained, but obviously uncowed and unbeaten, with his chin held high and his shoulders back.

"Welcome to Hollywood," L.M. said. "Sit down—give him a drink, Barney—and make yourself comfortable. What did you say your name was . . . ?"

"He doesn't speak English, L.M."

L.M. Greenspan's face fell. "I can't say I approve of that, Barney. I don't like working through interpreters, too slow, not reliable. . . . All right Lyn, do your stuff, ask him his name."

Jens Lyn mumbled to himself for a moment, going through the Old Norse verb forms, then spoke aloud. *"Hvat heitir maorinn?"*[3]

---

[1] "What is your name?"

The Viking only rumbled deep in his throat and ignored the question.

"What's the trouble?" L.M. asked impatiently. "I thought you talked his lingo? Can't he understand you?"

"You must be patient, sir. Old Norse has been a dead language for almost a thousand years and we know of it only through the written word. Icelandic is the modern language that most closely resembles it so I am using the Icelandic intonation and pronunciation—"

"All right, all right. Lectures I don't need. Make him comfortable and oil him up with a few drinks and let's get rolling."

Tex pushed a chair against the back of the Viking's legs and he sat down, glaring. Barney took a bottle of Jack Daniels from the bar concealed by the fake Rembrandt and poured a highball glass half full. But when he held it out to the Viking the man jerked his head away and rattled the chains that bound his wrists.

"*Eitr!*"[2] he snarled.

"He thinks that you are trying to poison him," Lyn said.

"That's easy to take care of," Barney said, and raised the glass and took a long drink. This time the Viking allowed the glass to be put to his lips and began to drink, his eyes opening wider and wider as he drained it to the last drop.

"*Ooinn ok Fitalrigg!*"[3] he bellowed happily and shook the tears from his eyes.

"He should like it, at $7.25 a bottle, plus tax," L.M. said. "You can bet they don't have that kind of stuff where he comes from. Nor Lifebuoy neither. Ask him again about the name."

The Viking frowned with concentration while he listened to the question repeated in a variety of ways, and answered readily enough once he understood.

"Ottar," he said and looked at the bottle longingly.

"Now we're getting someplace," L.M. said and looked at the clock on his desk. "We're also getting onto four

2 "Poison!"
3 "Odin and Frigg." (King and Queen of the Norse gods.)

23

o'clock in the morning and I want to get things settled. Ask this Ottar about the rate of exchange—what kind of money do they have, Lyn?"

"Well—they barter mostly, but mention is made of the silver mark."

"That's what we want to know. How many marks to the dollar, and tell him not to give any fancy bank figures. I want the free market price, we've been had this way before, and I'll buy the marks in Tangier if I have to—"

Ottar bellowed and hurled himself out of the chair, knocking Barney into a row of potted plants, which collapsed under him, and grabbed up the bourbon bottle. He had it raised to his mouth when Tex hit him with the sap and he slumped unconscious to the floor.

"What's this?" L.M. shouted. "Murder in my own office? Crazy men I got enough of in the organization, so take this one back where he came from and find one that speaks English. I don't want any translators next time."

"But none of them speak English," Barney said crossly, pulling fragments of cactus from his sleeve.

"Then teach one—but no more crazy men."

4

Barney Hendrickson suppressed a groan, and the hand that raised the carton of black coffee to his lips tremored ever so slightly. He had forgotten how many hours—or centuries—it had been since he had had any sleep. One difficulty had followed another through the night, until the dawn of a new day brought its own problems. Dallas Levy's voice buzzed in the earpiece of the phone like an irritated wasp while Barney sipped his coffee.

"I agree, I agree, Dallas," he rasped in answer, his vocal cords eroded by three chain-smoked packs of cigarettes. "Just stick by him and keep him quiet, no one ever goes near those old storerooms . . . Well you've been on double time the last three hours . . . All right then, treble time now, I'll okay the vouchers. Just keep him locked up and quiet until we decide what to do with him. And tell Dr. Lyn to get up here as soon as he has finished talking to B.O. Plenty."

Barney hung up the phone and tried to concentrate on the budget sheet before him. So far most of the entries were followed by penciled question marks; this was going to be a hard picture to cost. And what would happen if the police got wind of the Viking locked up down below? Could he be charged with kidnapping someone who had been dead almost a thousand years? "The mind reels," he mumbled, and reached for the coffee again. Professor Hewett, still apparently as fresh as ever, paced back and forth the length of the office, spinning a pocket calculator and scribbling the results in a small notebook.

"Any results yet, Prof?" Barney asked. "Can we send anything bigger than that truck back in time?"

"Patience, you must learn patience. Nature yields up her secrets only with the greatest reluctance, and a misplaced decimal point can make disclosure impossible. There are many factors that enter the equations other than the accepted four dimensions of physical measurement in time. We must consider three additional dimensions, those of displacement in space, mass, a cumulative error, which I am of the opinion is caused by entropy—"

"Spare me the details, just the answer, that's all I want," His intercom buzzed and he told his secretary to show Dr. Lyn in. Lyn refused a cigarette and folded his long form into a chair.

"Out with the bad news," Barney said. "Unless that is your normal expression. No luck with the Viking?"

"As you say, no luck. There is a communication problem, you realize, since my command of Old Norse is far from perfect, which must be coupled with the fact that Ottar has little or no interest in what I am trying to discuss with him. However, I do feel that with the proper encouragement he could be convinced that he should learn English."

"Encouragement . . . ?"

"Money, or the eleventh-century equivalent. Like most Vikings he is very mercenary and will do almost anything to gain status and wealth, though of course he prefers to get it by battle and killing."

"Of course. We can pay him for taking his language lessons, bookkeeping has worked out a rate of exchange and it's all in our favor, but what about the time factor? Can you have him speaking English in two weeks?"

"Impossible! With a cooperative student this might be done, but not with Ottar. He is reluctant at best, in addition to the not considerable factor that he refuses to do anything until he is released."

"Not considerable!" Barney said, and had the sudden desire to tug at a fistful of his own hair. "I can just see the hairy nut with his meat ax on the corner of Hollywood and Vine. That's out!"

"If I might offer a suggestion," Professor Hewett said, stopping his pacing in front of Barney's desk. "If Dr. Lyn were to return with this aborigine to his own time there would be ample opportunity to teach him English in his own environment, which would both reassure and calm him."

"It would not reassure or calm me, Professor," Lyn said coldly. "Life in that particular era tends to be both brutish and short."

"I'm sure precautionary measures can be taken, Doctor," said Hewett, giving his calculator a quick spin. "I would think that the philological opportunities would far outweight the personal factor . . ."

"There is of course that," Lyn agreed, his unfocused eyes staring at nouns, roots, cases and genders long buried by time.

"Plus the important point that in this manner the time factor can be altered to suit our needs. Gentlemen, we can collapse or stretch time as we will! Dr. Lyn can have ten days, or ten months, or ten years, to teach the language to Ottar, and between the moment when we leave him in the Viking era and the moment when we see him again but a few minutes need have passed from our point of view."

"Two months will be adequate," Lyn snapped, "if you wish to take into consideration *my* point of view."

"It's agreed then," Barney said. "Lyn will go back with

the Viking and teach him English, and we'll arrive with the company two months later Viking-time to start the production rolling."

"I have not agreed," Lyn persisted. "There are dangers . . ."

"I wonder what it would feel like to be the world's single greatest authority on Old Norse?" Barney asked, having had some experience with the academic mind, and the wide-eyed expression on Lyn's face revealed that his shaft had sunk home. "Right. We'll work out the details later. Why don't you go see if you can explain this to Ottar. Mention money. We'll get him to sign a completion and penalties contract, so you'll be safe enough as long as he wants his pay."

"It might be possible," Lyn agreed, and Barney knew that he was hooked.

"Right then. You get down to Ottar and put the deal to him, and while you're getting his okay I'll have the contract department draw up one of their barely legal, lifetime-at-hard-labor contracts." He flipped on the intercom. "Put me through to contracts, will you, Betty. Has the Benzedrine arrived yet?"

"I called the dispensary an hour ago," the intercom squeaked.

"Well call them again if you expect me to live past noon."

As Jens Lyn went out, a slight Oriental wearing pink slacks, a cerise shirt, a Harris Tweed sports jacket and a sour expression entered.

"Well, Charley Chang," Barney boomed, sticking out his hand, "long time no see."

"It's been too long, Barney," Charley said, grinning widely and shaking the outstretched hand. "Good to work with you again."

They disliked each other intensely and as soon as their hands separated Barney lit a cigarette, and the smile vanished into the unhappy folds of Chang's normal expression. "What's cooking, Barney?" he asked.

"A wide-screen, three-hour, big-budget film—and you're the only man who can write it."

"We're running out of books, Barney, but I've always thought that there was a good one in the Song of Solomon, sexy without being dirty—"

"The subject has already been chosen, a wholly new concept of the Viking discoveries of North America."

Chang's frown deepened. "Sounds good, Barney, but you know I'm a specialist. I don't think this is up my alley."

"You're a good writer, Charley, which means everything is up your alley. Besides, ha-ha, let's not forget your contract," he added, slipping the dagger a few inches out of the scabbard so it could be seen.

"No, we can't forget the contract, ha-ha," Charley said coldly. "I've always been interested in doing a historical."

"That's great," Barney said, pulling the budget sheet toward him again. The door opened and a messenger pushed in a trolley loaded with books. Barney pointed at them. "Here's the scoop from the library, everything you need to know. Just take a quick flip through them and I'll be with you in a minute."

"A minute, sure, sure," Charlie said, looking coldly at the twenty-odd thick volumes.

"Five thousand seven hundred and seventy-three point two eight cubic meters with a loading of twelve thousand seven hundred and seventy-seven point six two kilograms at a power increase of twenty-seven point two per cent," Professor Hewett suddenly said.

"What the hell are you talking about?" Barney snapped.

"Those are the figures you asked for, the size of load the vremeatron will be able to handle with an increased power supply."

"Very nice. Now will you translate it into American."

"Roughly speaking"—Hewett rolled his eyes up and mumbled quickly under his breath—"I would say that a fourteen-ton load could be temporally moved, measuring twelve feet by twelve feet by forty feet."

"That's more like it. That should hold anything we might possibly need."

"Contract," Betty said, dropping an eight-page multifolded document onto his desk.

28

"All right," Barney said, slipping quickly through the crisp sheets. "Get Dallas Levy up here."

"Miss Tove is waiting outside to see you."

"Not now! Tell her my leprosy is acting up. And where are those bennies? I'm not going to get through this morning on coffee alone."

"I've rung the dispensary three more times, there seems to be something about a staff shortage today."

"Those unfeeling bastards. You better get down there and bring them back yourself."

"Why Barney Hendrickson—it must have been *years* . . ."

The hoarse-voiced words hurtled across the office and left silence in their wake. Gossipmongers said that Slithey Tove had the acting ability of a marionette with loose strings, the brain of a chihuahua and the moral standards of Fanny Hill. They were right. Yet these qualities, or lack of qualities, did not explain the success of her pictures. The one quality that Slithey did have, in overabundance, was femaleness, plus the ability to communicate on what must have been a hormone level. She did not generate an aura of sex, but rather one of sexual availability. Which was true enough. This aura was strong enough to carry, scarcely diminished, through all the barriers of film, lenses and projectors to radiate, hot and steaming, from the silver screen. Her pictures made money. Most women didn't like them. Her aura, now operating unhampered by time, space or celluloid, swept the room like a sensual sonar, clicking with passion unrestrained.

Betty sniffed loudly and swept out of the room, though she had to slow momentarily to get past the actress, who stood sideways in the doorway. It was said, truthfully, that Slithey had the largest bust in Hollywood.

"Slithey . . ." Barney said, and his voice cracked. Too many cigarettes, of course.

"Barney darling . . ." she said, as the smoothly hydraulic pistons of her rounded legs propelled her slowly across the office, "it's been ages since I've *seen* you."

With her hands on the desk top, she leaned forward and gravity tugged down at the thin fabric of her blouse and at least 98 per cent of her bosom swam into view. Barney felt

29

he was flying upside down into a fleshy Grand Canyon.

"Slithey," Barney said, springing suddenly to his feet: he had almost fallen into this trap before. "I want to talk to you about this picture we're planning, but you see I'm busy just now . . ."

Inadvertently he had taken her arm—which throbbed like a great, hot, beating heart under his fingers as she leaned close. He snatched his hand away.

"If you'll just hold on a bit, I'll be with you as soon as I can."

"I'll just sit over there against the wall," the husky voice said. "I know I won't be in the way."

"You want me?" Dallas Levy asked from the open doorway, talking to Barney while his eyes made a careful survey of the actress. Hormone contacted hormone and she inhaled automatically. He slowly smiled.

"Yes," Barney said, digging the contract out of the litter of papers on his desk. "Take this down to Lyn and tell him to get his friend to sign it. Any trouble?"

"Not since we found out he likes burnt beefsteak and beer. Anytime he starts acting up we slip him another steak and a quart of beer and he forgets his troubles. Eight steaks and eight quarts so far."

"Get that signature," Barney said, and his gaze fell accidentally on Slithey, who had oozed into the armchair and crossed her silk-shod legs. Her garters had little pink bows on them. . . .

"What do you say, Charley?" Barney asked, collapsing into his swivel chair and spinning it about. "Any ideas yet?"

Charley Chang raised the thick volume he held in both hands. "I'm on page thirteen of this one and there are a few more books to go."

"Background material," Barney told him. "We can rough out the main story lines now and you can fill in the details later. L.M. suggested a saga, and we can't go wrong with that. We open in the Orkney Islands around the year 1000 when there is plenty of trouble. You have Norse settlers and Viking raiders and things are really hotting up. Maybe you open with a Viking raid, the dragon ship gliding across the dark waters, you know."

"Like opening a Western with the bankrobbers silently riding into town?"

"That's the idea. The hero is the chief Viking, or maybe the head man ashore, you'll work that out. So there's some fighting, then some more of the same, so the hero decides to move his bunch to the new world, Vinland, which he has just heard about."

"Like the winning of the West?"

"Right. Then the voyage, the storm, the shipwreck, the landing, the first settlement, the battle with the Indians. Think big because we're going to have plenty of extras. End on a high note, looking into the sunset."

Charley Chang scribbled notes on the flyleaf of the book as Barney talked, nodding his head in agreement. "Just one thing more," he said, holding up the book. "Some of the names of the guys in this book are really a gas. Listen to this, here's one called Eyjolf the Foul, who has a friend name of Hergil Hnappraz. And Polarbear Pig, Ragnar Hairybreeks—a million more. We could play this for laughs . . . ?"

"This is a serious film, Charley, just as serious as any you have ever done from—"

"You're the boss, Barney. Just a suggestion. But what about the love interest?"

"Work her in early, you know how to do it."

"That role is made for *me,* Barney darling," the voice whispered in his ear as warm arms wrapped him and he began to drown in a sea of resilient flesh.

"Don't let him sweet-talk you, Slithey," he heard a muffled voice say. "Barney Hendrickson is my buddy, indeed my old buddy, but a mighty good businessman to boot, shrewd, so no matter what you promise him, I'm sorry to have to say this, I gotta look closely at all contracts before we sign."

"Ivan," Barney said, struggling free of the perfumed octopoid embrace, "just take your client aside for a moment then I'll be with you. I don't know if we can do business, but at least we can talk."

Ivan Grissini, who, despite the fact that his lank hair, hawk nose and rumpled, dandruff-speckled suit made him look like a crooked agent, was a crooked agent. He could smell a deal ten miles upwind in a hailstorm and always carried sixteen fountain pens that he filled ritually each morning before leaving for the office.

"Sit over here, baby," he said, levering Slithey toward the corner with a long-practiced motion. Since she wasn't stuffed with greenbacks he was immune to her charms. "Barney Hendrickson is a man good as his word, even better."

The phone rang just as Jens Lyn came in waving the contract. "Ottar cannot sign this," he said. "It is in English."

"Well translate it, you're the technical adviser. Hold on." He picked up the phone.

"I could translate it, it would be extremely difficult but possible, but what would be the point? He cannot read."

"Just hold on, Lyn. No, not you, Sam. I know, Sam . . . Of course I saw the estimate, I made it myself. No, you don't have to ask me where I'm getting the LSD . . . Be realistic yourself. Yesterday neither of us was born not, I agree . . . what you don't realize is that this picture can be produced within the figure I outlined, give or take fifty thousand . . . Don't use the word impossible, Sam. The impossible may take a while, but we do it, you know the routine . . . What? . . . On the phone? Sam, be reasonable. I've got three rings of Barnum and Bailey in the office right now, this isn't the time to go into details . . . Brushoff? Me? Never! . . . Yes, by all means, ask him. L.M. has been in on this picture from the beginning, every step of the way, and you'll find that he'll back me up in my own footsteps every step of the way . . . Right . . . And the same to you, Sam."

He dropped the phone into the cradle and Charley Chang said, "She could be captured in the raid, in the opening, she could fight with him with true hatred, but hatred would, in spite of itself, turn to love."

"I've *never* been captured in a raid before," Slithey husked from the corner.

"A good idea, Charley," Barney agreed.

"And even if he could read—he cannot write," Lyn said.

"We've had that problem with foreign actors more than

32

once," Barney told him. "Staple the true translation to the contract, have it notarized as a true translation by a bilingual notary, have the party of the second part make his mark and affix his thumb print on each document, both witnessed by two impartial witnesses, and it will stand up in any court in the world."

"There may be some difficulty in locating a bilingual English-Old Norse notary—"

"Ask casting, they can find anyone."

"Here they are, Mr. Hendrickson," his secretary said, coming in through the open door and placing a bottle of Benzedrine tablets before him on the desk.

"Too late," Barney whispered, staring at them, unmoving. "Too late."

The telephone and the intercom sounded at the same moment and he groped out two of the pills and washed them down with the cold, black, cardboardy coffee.

"Hendrickson here," he said flipping the key.

"Barney, I would like to see you in my office at once," L.M.'s voice said.

Betty had answered the phone. "That was L.M. Greenspan's secretary," she said. "L.M. would like to see you in his office at once."

"I get the message."

His thigh muscles hurt when he stood up and he wondered how long it would take for the bennies to show some effect. "Stay with it, Charley, I'll want a synopsis, a couple of sheets, as soon as possible."

When he started toward the door Ivan Grissini's hand darted toward his lapel, but he moved away from it with reflex efficiency. "Stick around, Ivan, I'll want to talk to you after I see L.M." The chorus of voices was cut off as he closed the door behind him. "Lend me your towel, will you, Betty," he asked.

She took the towel from the bottom drawer of her desk and he draped it around his shoulders, tucking it carefully inside the collar of his shirt. Then he bent and placed his head under the faucet of the water cooler and gasped when Betty turned it on. He let the icy stream run over his head and the back of his neck for a few moments, then straightened up and dried himself off. Betty lent him her comb. He felt weaker but better, and when he looked in the mirror he looked almost human. Almost.

"Lock the door behind you," L.M. said when Barney came into the office, then grunted as he bent over to clip a telephone wire with a pair of angle-nose wire cutters. "Are there any more, Sam?"

"That's the last one," Sam said in his gray, colorless voice. Sam was pretty much of a gray, colorless man, which was assuredly protective coloration since he was L.M.'s own personal, private accountant and was reputed to be a world authority on corporative finance and tax evasion. He clutched a folder of papers protectively to his chest and flicked his eyes toward L.M. "That is no longer necessary," he said.

"Maybe, maybe," L.M. said, puffing as he fell into his chair. "But if I even say the word *bank* when the wires aren't cut my heart gives palpitations. I got not so good news for you, Barney." He bit off the end of a cigar. "We're ruined."

"What do you mean?" Barney looked back and forth from one expressionless face to the other. "Is this some kind of gag?"

"What L.M. means," Sam said, "is that Climactic Studios will soon be bankrupt."

"On the rocks, the work of a lifetime," L.M. said in a hollow voice.

Sam nodded once, as mechanically as a ventriloquist's dummy, and said, "That is, roughly, the situation. Normally it would be at least three more months before our financial report would be sent to the banks, who, as you know, own the controlling percentage of this corporation. However, for some reason unknown to us, they are sending their accountants to examine the books this week."

"And . . . ?" Barney asked, feeling suddenly lightheaded. The silence lengthened unbearably until he jumped to his feet and began to pace the room. "And they'll find the company is on the rocks, and that all the profits are on paper"—he turned and pointed dramatically to L.M.—"and that all the hard cash has been bled off into the untaxable L.M. Greenspan Foundation. No wonder you're not suffering. The company may go down the drain, but L.M. Greenspan goes marching on."

"Watch it! That's no way for an employee to talk to the man who gave him his first break—"

"And his last one too—right here!" Barney said, and chopped himself on the neck with the edge of his hand, much harder than he had planned. "Listen, L.M.," he pleaded, rubbing the sore spot, "until the ax falls we still have a chance. You must have thought there was the possibility of a salvage operation or you wouldn't have got involved in this deal with Professor Hewett and his machine. You must have felt that a big box-office success would get the pressure off, make the firm solvent again. We can still do it."

L.M. shook his head morosely. "Don't think it doesn't hurt to shake hands with the knife that stabs you in the back, but what else can I do? A big box-office hit, sure, even a big picture in the can and we could laugh at the teeth of the banks. But you can't make a picture in a week."

You can't make a picture in a week! The words hissed and sizzled through the caffeine-clogged, Benzedrine-loaded channels of Barney's brain, levering up a reluctant memory.

"L.M." he said dramatically. "You're going to have a heart attack."

"Bite your tongue!" L.M. gasped, and clutched a roll of fat roughly near that vital organ. "Don't say that. One coronary's enough to last a lifetime."

."Listen to this. You go home with Sam to work on the books tonight, you take them with you. You get sick. It could be indigestion, it could be a coronary. Your doctor says it could be a coronary. The fees you've been paying him he should deliver at least that one small favor. Everyone runs around and shouts for a few days and the books are forgotten about and then it is the weekend, and nobody even considers looking at the books until Monday, maybe Tuesday."

"Monday," Sam said firmly. "You don't know banks. No books on Monday and they'll have a hired car full of doctors over to the house."

"All right, Monday then. That will be time enough."

"So Monday—but what difference does it make? Frankly, I'm puzzled," L.M. said, and knitted his brow and looked puzzled.

"It makes this difference, L.M. On Monday I will bring you the new picture in the can. A picture that will have to gross two, three million on length, width of screen and color alone."

"But you can't!"

"But we can. You're forgetting about the vremeatron. This gadget works. Remember last night when you thought we had all gone for about ten minutes?" L.M. nodded reluctantly. "That was how long we were gone from here and now. But we were an hour or more in the Viking times. We could do it again. Take the company and everything we need back there to shoot the picture, and use just as much time as we need to do it right before we came back."

"You mean . . . ?"

"Correct. When we come back with the film in the can we need only have been gone *ten minutes* as far as you're concerned."

"Why didn't they ever think of this before?" L.M. gasped with happy appreciation.

"For a lot of reasons . . ."

"Do you mean to tell me . . ." Sam leaned so far forward in his chair that he was almost out of it, and the hint of some expression, perhaps a smile?, touched his face. "Do you mean that we will have to pay production costs for just *ten minutes?*"

"I do not mean that," Barney snapped. "I can tell you in advance that there are going to be some headaches for bookkeeping. However, to cheer you up, I can guarantee that we can shoot on location—with more extras—for about one-tenth the cost of filming in Spain."

Sam's eyes glittered. "I don't know the details of this project, L.M., but some of the factors make very good sense."

"Can you do it, Barney? Pull this thing off?"

"I can do it if you give me all the help I ask for and no questions. This is Tuesday. I see no reason why we can't have everything we need sewn up by Saturday." He

36

counted off on his fingers. "We'll have to get the contracts signed with the principals, get enough raw film to last for all the shooting, the technicians, at least two extra cameras . . ." He began to mumble to himself as he ran through all they might possibly need. "Yes," he said finally, "we can do it."

"Still, I don't know," L.M. said pensively. "It's a wild idea."

The future teetered on the balance and Barney groped desperately for inspiration.

"Just one more thing," he said. "If we're on location for, say, six months, everyone has to be paid six months' salary. But we rent the cameras and sound equipment, all of the expensive hardware, we will only have to pay for a few *days* rental fees for them."

"Barney," L.M. said, sitting up straight in his chair, "you've got yourself a deal."

5

"You haven't heard the last of Cinecittà yet, Mr. Hendrickson."

"Barney."

"Not yet, Barney, not by a long shot. The new realism came out of Italy after the war, then the kitchen-sink film that the British picked up. But you'll see, Rome ain't dead yet. Guys like me come over here to Hollywood for a bit, pick up some techniques—"

"Pick up some loot."

". . . can't deny that, Barney, working for the Yankee dollar. But you know, you're not going to get much on color this time of day." He swung the 8-mm Bolex that hung on a thong from his wrist. "I should have loaded this up with Tri-X. It's five in the afternoon."

"Don't worry, Gino, you'll have plenty of light, take my word for that." He looked up as the warehouse door opened and Amory Blestead came in. "Over here,

Amory," he said. "This is our cameraman, Gino Cappo. Amory Blestead, technical adviser."

"Pleased to meet you," Amory said, shaking hands, "I always wondered how you got those repulsive effects in *Autumn Love*."

"You mean in *Porco Mondo?* Those weren't effects, that's just the way that part of Yugoslavia looks."

"Christ!" He turned to Barney. "Dallas told me to tell you they'll be down with Ottar in about five minutes."

"About time. We'll have the Prof warm his machine up."

Barney climbed painfully into the back of the army truck and dropped onto the boxes. He had managed to grab about an hour's sleep on the couch in his office before another urgent message from L.M. had dragged him awake and up to L.M.'s office for an extended wrangle over budgeting. The pace was beginning to tell.

"I have recalibrated all my instruments," Professor Hewett said, tapping happily on a dial face, "so that now I can guarantee the utmost precision temporally and geographically in all future time transports."

"Wonderful. See if you can recalibrate us to arrive just after our last trip, close to the same time, the same day. The light was good—"

The door crashed open, and loud, guttural singing filled the warehouse. Ottar stumbled in with Jens Lyn and Dallas Levy each clutching one of his arms, holding him up rather than restraining him, since he was obviously roaring drunk. Tex Antonelli came behind them wheeling a handtruck loaded with packing cases. It needed all three of them to heave the Viking up into the truck, where he passed out, mumbling happily to himself. They piled the boxes in around him.

"What's all this?" Barney asked.

"Trade goods," Lyn said, pushing the crate labeled JACK DANIELS in over the tailgate. "Ottar signed the contract. I was very surprised to discover an Icelandic notary public here—"

"You can find anything in Hollywood."

"And Ottar agreed to study English once he was back in his own house. He has developed a decided taste for
38

distilled beverages and we agreed on a payment of one bottle of whiskey a day for every day of study."

"Couldn't you have fobbed him off with some rotgut?" Barny asked as a second crate of Jack Daniels slid into the truck. "I can see myself trying to justify this on the gyp sheet."

"We did try," Dallas said, shoving in a third case. "Slipped him some Old Overcoat 95 per cent grain neutral spirits, but it was no sale. He developed an educated palate early. Two months, five cases, that's the bargain."

Jens Lyn climbed in and Barney admired his knee-high engineer's boots, puttees, many-pocketed hunting jacket and sheath knife. "Why the Jungle Jim outfit?" he asked.

"A simple matter of survival and creature comfort," Lyn said, making room for the sleeping bag and a packing crate that Dallas pushed up to him. "I have DDT for the body lice that are sure to abound, halazone tablets for the drinking water and a quantity of tinned food. The diet of the time is restricted, and I am sure unwholesome to modern tastes. Therefore I have taken a few simple precautions."

"Fair enough," Barney said. "Climb in and lock up the tailgate, let's get rolling."

Though the vremeatron still whined and crackled with the same intensity, there was no longer the tension there had been on the first trip. The conditioned reflexes of mechanized man took over and the voyage through time became just as commonplace as a ride in a high-speed elevator, a trip in a jet plane, a descent in a submarine or a blast-off in a rocket. Only Gino, the newcomer, showed some apprehension, darting rapid glances at the bank of electronic gadgetry and the sealed warehouse. But in the face of the others' calm—Barney managed to doze off during the transition while Dallas and the Danish philologist quarreled over the opening of one of the whiskey bottles and the resultant loss thereby of a day's English lessons—he relaxed a little. When the transition did occur he half rose, startled, but sat down again when the bottle was passed to him, though his eyes did widen considerably when the ice-blue sky appeared outside and the tang of salt spray filled the truck.

"That's a pretty good trick," he said, pointing his light meter. "How's it done?"

"For details you have to ask the Prof here," Barney said, gasping over too large a swallow of the whiskey. "Very complex. Something about moving through time."

"I get it," Gino said, stopping his diaphragm down to 3.5. "Something like the time zones when you fly from London to New York. The sun doesn't seem to move and you arrive at the same time you took off."

"Something like that."

"Good light. We can get some good color with light like this."

"If you drive don't drink," Dallas said, leaning out to hand the bottle to Tex, who sat behind the wheel in the cab. "One slug and let's get on the trail, pardner."

The starter whined the motor to life and, looking out over the cab, Barney saw that they were following the tire tracks of another truck, clearly visible in the damp sand and gravel. Memory pushed up through the layers of fatigue and he hammered on the metal roof of the cab over Tex's head.

"Blow your horn," he shouted.

They were coming to the rocky headland and the horn sounded as they swung around it. Barney stumbled over the crates and trod on the sleeping Viking as he rushed to the rear of the truck. There was the rising grumble of another engine as an identical army truck passed them, going in the opposite direction. Barney reached the open rear and clutched the bent-wood canvas support over his head. He had a quick glimpse of himself in the rear of the other truck, white-faced and wide-eyed and gaping like a moron. With a feeling of sadomasochistic pleasure he raised his open hand, thumb to nose, and wiggled his fingers at his shocked other self. The rock headland came in between them.

"Get much traffic around here?" Gino asked.

Ottar sat up, rubbing his side, muttering something foul under his breath. Jens quieted him easily with a long drag from the bottle as they braked to a sliding stop in the loose gravel.

"Primrose Cottage," Tex shouted back, "last stop."

Reeking smoke still drifted down from the chimney hole of the squat, turf house, but there was no one in sight. Weapons and clumsy tools littered the ground. Ottar half fell, half jumped from the truck and bellowed something, then clutched at his head with instant regret.

"Hvar erut per rakka? Komit út!"[1] He held his head again and looked around for the bottle, which Jens Lyn had wisely tucked out of sight. The servants began tremblingly to appear.

"Let's get moving," Barney said. "Get these cases unloaded and ask Dr. Lyn where he wants them. Not you, Gino, I want you to come with me."

They climbed the low hill behind the house, pushing through the short, stubbly grass and almost tripping over a ragged and wild-looking sheep that went baaing down the hill away from them. From the top they had a clear view of the curving bay that swept away from them on both sides, and the vast, slate-gray ocean. A long roller came in, breaking up on the beach, then hissing away again through the pebbles. A grim-looking island with cliff sides that fell straight to the foaming ocean stood in the middle of the bay, and farther off, just a dark blur on the horizon, was another, lower island.

"Pan right around in a circle, 360 degrees, so we can study it later. Zoom in for a close-up on that island."

"What about going inland a bit, take a look at the land there?" Gino asked, squinting through the viewfinder.

"Later, if there's time. But this is going to be a sea picture and with all this free ocean I want to use it."

"Along the shore then, we should see what's behind the point there."

"That's all right—but don't go alone. Take Tex or Dallas with you so you stay out of trouble. Don't get more than a fifteen-minute walk away, so we can find you when we have to leave." Barney glanced along the shore and noticed the rowboat; he took Gino's arm and pointed. "There's an idea. Get Lyn to translate and have a couple of the locals row you offshore a bit. Give me some shots of the way this place looks coming in from the sea . . ."

[1] "Where are you, dogs? Come out!"

"Hey," Tex said, pulling himself over the brow of the hill, "they want you down at the shack, Barney. Pow-wow of some kind."

"Just in time, Tex. Stay with Gino here and keep an eye on him."

"I'll stick to him like glue. *'Va buona, eh cumpa'?*"

Gino shot him a dark, suspicious look. "*Vui sareste italiano?*"

Tex laughed. "Me? No, I'm *Americano,* but I got ginzo relatives all around the Bay of Naples."

"*Di Napoli! so' napoletano pur'io!*" Gino shouted happily.

Barney left them enthusiastically pumping hands and discovering mutual relations, and went down to the house. Dallas was sitting on the tailgate of the truck smoking a cigarette held in his cupped hand. "The rest of them are inside," he said, "and I'm keeping an eye on the shop to make sure we got transportation home. Lyn said to send you in when you come."

Barney looked at the low door of the house with complete lack of enthusiasm. It stood partly open and more smoke appeared to be coming from it than was coming out of the chimney. "See that you do watch it," he said. "I can think of a lot more attractive spots to be shipwrecked."

"The same idea had occurred to me," Dallas said quietly and lifted his other hand to show the automatic pistol he was holding. "Ten shots. I never miss."

Pushing the door wide, Barney stooped and entered the house. The smoke from the smouldering fire was thick around his head, and he was almost grateful, since it served to mask some of the other odors that hung richly in the air. He recognized old fish, tar, locker-room lilac, plus others that he did not want to recognize. For the moment he was almost blind, coming in out of the sun, since the only light here came through the door and some openings that had apparently been kicked in the wall.

"*Jaeja, kunningi! pu skalt drekka meo mér!*"[2]

Ottar's hoarse voice shivered the air, and, as his eyes adjusted a bit, Barney could make out the men seated

[2] "Ho, my friend! You shall drink with me!"

around a thick plank table, with Ottar at one end hammering on the boards with his fist.

"He wants you to join him in a drink," Lyn said. "This is a very important step, hospitality, bread and salt, that sort of thing."

"*Ol!*"[3] Ottar bellowed, picking a small barrel up from the stamped earth floor.

"Drink what?" Barney asked, frowning into the darkness.

"Ale. They make it from barley, their staple crop. It is an invention of these north Germanic tribes, the ancestor you might say of our modern beer. Even the word has come down to us, though slightly changed in pronunciation of course—"

"*Drekk!*"[4] Ottar ordered as he slopped full a horn and handed it to Barney. It really was a cow's horn, Barney saw, curved and cracked and none too clean. Jens Lyn, the professor and Amory Blestead were also clutching horns. He raised it to his lips and took a sip. It was flat, sour, watery and tasted terrible.

"Good," he said, hoping his expression could not be seen in the darkness.

"*Já, gott ok vel,*"[5] Ottar agreed and poured more of the loathsome beverage into Barney's cup so that it slopped over and ran stickily down his arm inside his sleeve.

"If you think that's bad," Amory said hollowly, "wait until you taste the food."

"And here it comes now."

The professor pointed to the end of the room where one of the servants was rooting about in a large wooden chest against the wall. As he straightened up, the man kicked one of the rounded dark mounds that littered the floor there and a pained lowing trembled the air.

"The livestock . . . ?" Barney could not finish.

"Kept in the house, that's right," Amory said. "That's what adds a certain, subtle fragrance to the air in here."

The servant, who looked not unlike an uncurried sheep-

[3] "Ale!"
[4] "Drink!"
[5] "Yes, very good,"

43

dog, with his long blond hair that fell down and concealed his eyes, trudged over with a lumpish object clutched in each grimy paw and dropped them onto the table before Barney. They cracked against the wood like falling rocks.

"What's this?" Barney asked, eyeing them suspiciously out of the corner of his eye as he transferred the horn to his other hand and tried to shake the rivulet of ale out of the sleeve of his cashmere jacket.

"The chunk on the left is cheese, a native product, and the other is *knaekbrød,* hard bread," Jens Lyn said. "Or is it the other way around?"

Barney tried a nibble of each, or rather clattered his teeth against them, in turn. "That's great, really great," he said, throwing them back onto the table and looking at the glowing dial of his watch. "The light's going and we should start back soon. I want to talk to you, Amory, outside, if you can tear yourself away from the party."

"My pleasure," Amory said, shuddering as he finished most of his horn, then turned the thick dregs out onto the floor.

The sun had dropped behind an icy band of cloud and a cold breeze was blowing in from the sea; Barney shivered and pushed his hands into his jacket pockets.

"I need your help, Amory," he said. "Draw up a list of everything we're going to need to shoot this picture on location here. It doesn't look as though we'll be able to help ourselves locally with any commissary supplies—"

"Second that motion!"

"So we'll have to bring it all with us. I want to do all the cutting here, so set up a cutting room in one of the trailers."

"You're looking for trouble, Barney. It will be a devil of a job to turn out even a rough cut here. And what about dubbing? Or the musical score?"

"We'll do the best we can. Hire a composer and couple of musicians, maybe use a local orchestra."

"I can hear *that* already."

"It doesn't matter if we have to dub most of the sound again. What does matter is bringing back the film in the can . . ."

"Mr. Hendrickson," Jens Lyn called, pushing open the

door and coming toward them. He fumbled in the breast pocket of his bush jacket. "I just remembered, there was a message I was supposed to give you."

"What is it?" Barney asked.

"I have no idea. I presumed it was confidential. Your secretary handed it to me just as we were leaving."

Barney took the crumpled envelope and tore it open. It contained a single sheet of yellow paper with a brief, typed message. It read:

> L.M. on phone says cancel
> operation, all work to cease on
> picture. No reason given.

6

Barney threw the magazine back onto the table, but the cover stuck to his hand and half tore off. He impatiently peeled away the paper and regretted not having taken the time to wash off the Viking beer before coming here. But *canceled!*

"Miss Zucker," he said. "L.M. wants to see me. He said so. He left a message. I'm sure that he is waiting impatiently to hear from me . . ."

"I'm very sorry, Mr. Hendrickson, but he left strictest instructions that he is in conference and cannot be disturbed." Her fingers poised for a second over the typewriter, her gum-chewing suspended momentarily. "I will notify him that you are waiting as soon as I am able." The typewriter thrummed again, the jaws moving in slow rhythm with it.

"You could at least ring through and tell him that I'm here."

"Mr. Hendrickson!" she said, her tones those a Mother Superior might use if accused of running a bawdy house.

Barney went over and took a drink of water from the cooler, then rinsed off his sticky hand. He was drying it on some typing paper when the intercom buzzed and Miss Zucker nodded to him. "You may go in now," she said coldly.

"What do you mean, L.M.?" he asked the instant the door closed behind him. "What do you mean by sending me that message?" Sam sat propped in his chair as mobile as a log of wood and Charley Chang slumped across from him, sweating heavily and looking miserable.

"What do I mean? What could I possibly mean I mean? I mean you led me up the garden path, Barney Hendrickson, and pulled my leg. You got my agreement to go ahead on a picture when you *didn't even have a script!*"

"Of course I don't have a script, how could I when we just decided to do the picture. This is an emergency, remember?"

"How could I forget. But an emergency is one thing, doing a picture without a script is another. In France maybe, they make the arty-schmarty things you couldn't tell if they had a script or not. But in Climactic we don't work that way."

"It's not good business," Sam agreed.

Barney tried not to wring his hands. "L.M., look. Be reasonable. This is a salvage operation, have you forgotten that? There are very *special circumstances* involved—"

"Say *bank*. The word don't hurt no more."

"I won't say it, because we can beat them yet. We can make this picture. So you called in my scriptwriter—"

"He got no script."

"Of course he's got no script. It was just yesterday when you and I finalized the idea. Now you've talked to him and explained your ideas—"

"He got no script."

"Hear me out, L.M. Charley's a good man, you picked him yourself and you briefed him yourself. If any man can deliver the goods, good old Charley can. If you had a Charley Chang script in your hand for this film you would let production go ahead, wouldn't you?"

"He got no—"

"L.M., you're not listening. *If.* That's the big word. If I were to here and now hand you a Charley Chang script for

46

this great motion picture titled . . . titled . . . *Viking Columbus*, would you okay production?"

L.M. was wearing his best poker face. He glanced over at Sam, who let his head drop the merest fraction of an inch. "Yes," L.M. instantly said.

"We're halfway home, L.M.," Barney hurried on. "If I were to hand you that script just one hour from now, you would okay production. Same difference, right?"

L.M. shrugged. "All right, same difference. But what difference does it make?"

"Sit right there, L.M.," Barney said, grabbing the startled Charley Chang by the arm and dragging him from the room. "Talk to Sam about the budget, have a drink—and I'll see you in exactly one hour. *Viking Columbus* is almost ready to roll."

"My head shrinker keeps evening hours," Charley said when the door closed behind him. "Let him talk to you, Barney. I have heard rash promises in this rash business many, many times, but this takes the gold plated bagel—"

"Save it, Charley. You got some work ahead of you." Barney steered the reluctant script writer out into the corridor while he talked. "Just give me your estimate of how long it would take you to rough out a first draft of a script for this film, working hard and putting your best into it. How long?"

"It's a big job. At least six months."

"Right. Six weeks. Concentrated effort, a first-class job."

"I said *months*. And even six weeks are more than an hour."

"If you need six months you can have them. You have all the time you need, just take my word for it. And a nice quiet spot to work." They were passing a photomural and Barney stopped and jabbed his thumb against it. "There. Santa Catalina Island. Plenty of sun, a refreshing dip in the briny when the thoughts grow stale."

"I can't work there. It's lousy with people, parties all night."

"That's what you think. How would you like to work on Catalina without another soul around, the whole island to yourself? Just think of the work you could get done."

47

"Barney, honestly, I don't know what the hell you are talking about."

"You will, Charley. In a very few minutes you will."

"Fifty reams of typing paper, a box of carbon paper, typing chair—one, typing table—one, typewriter . . ."

"This is a steam model, Barney," Charley said. "The antique kind you push with the fingers. I can only work with an IBM electric."

"I'm afraid the electric current isn't so reliable on the part of the island where you'll be. You watch how fast the fingers will get the old touch back." Barney made a tick mark on the sheet as a big crate was pushed into the back of the truck. "One safari outfit, complete."

"One *what?*"

"A do-it-yourself safari from the prop department. Tent, cots, mosquito nets, chairs, folding kitchen—and everything works. You'll feel just like Dr. Livingstone only twice as comfortable. Fifty-gallon drum of water —three, spring-powered time clock with cards—one."

Charley Chang watched in numb incomprehension as the varied assortments of items was loaded into the army truck. None of it made any sense, including the old geezer behind all the junk who was working away on a Frankenstein radio set. The ancient, mahogany time clock with roman numerals on its face was pushed over the tailgate, and Charley grabbed Barney's arm and pointed to it.

"None of this do I understand, and that least of all. Why a time clock?"

"Professor Hewett will explain everything in greatest detail in a few minutes, meanwhile take it all on faith. The clock is an important part, you'll see. Punch in every morning, don't forget."

"Mr. Hendrickson," his secretary called out, "you're very much in luck." She came into the warehouse leading by the arm a frowning Negro who wore white work clothes and a tall chef's hat. "You said you wanted a cook, but instantly, and I went right to our commissary and found Clyde Rawlston here. Not only can he cook, but he can take shorthand and type."

"You're an angel, Betty. Order another typewriter . . ."

48

"It's on the way. Did the first-aid box come?"

"Already aboard. That's the lot then. Clyde this is Charley, Charley, Clyde. You'll get better acquainted later. If you will kindly board the truck now."

"I'll go as soon as someone explains what is going on around here," Clyde Rawlston said with cold-eyed belligerence.

"A company emergency, Climactic needs you, and as loyal employees I know you'll both cooperate. Professor Hewett will explain it all to you. It won't take long. I'll see you both right here in just ten minutes by my watch, that's a promise. Now—if you will just climb over those crates so I can get this tailgate up."

Chivvied on by the voice of authority, they clambered aboard and Professor Hewett leaned out over their shoulders.

"I thought the Cambrian period would be best," he said to Barney. "You know, early Paleozoic. A nice, moderate climate, warm and comfortable, with no vertebrates around to cause trouble. Seas churning with the simple trilobite. Though it might be a little warm for continued comfort. Perhaps a little later in the Devonian. There would still be nothing big enough to harm—"

"You're the doctor, Prof, whatever you think best. We have to work fast now, at least on this end. Take them to Catalina, drop them off, then move six weeks ahead and bring them back here. Leave the junk on the island, we may need it later. Only about fifteen minutes left."

"Consider it done. With each trip made I feel it easier to calibrate the instruments, so that now the settings are most precise. No time shall be wasted, no time at all."

Professor Hewett returned to his instruments and the generator howled. Charley Chang was trying to say something, but his words were cut off as the truck vanished. There was no flicker or fading, it just disappeared as instantly and as quickly as the image on a back-projection screen when the film breaks. Barney started to turn to talk to his secretary, but just as his motion began the truck reappeared.

"What's wrong?" he asked, then saw that all the supplies were gone from the back. Clyde Rawlston was standing near the professor at the controls and Charley Chang was sitting on an empty crate clutching a thick folder of typed sheets.

"Nothing is wrong," the professor said. "I have just timed our return with the utmost of exact precision."

Charley was no longer wearing his jacket and his shirt was creased and faded, so bleached by the sun across the shoulders that all the color was gone. His hair was long and a black bristle of beard covered his cheeks.

"How did it go?" Barney asked.

"Not bad—considering. I'm not quite finished though, you see it's those things in the water. Those teeth! Eyes . . . !"

"How much more time do you need?"

"Two weeks should wrap it up, with time to spare. But, Barney, the eyes . . ."

"There's nothing there big enough to hurt you, that's what the Prof said."

"Maybe not big, but in the ocean, so many of them, and the teeth . . ."

"See you. Take it away, Prof. Two weeks."

This time the truck barely flickered, and if he had blinked at the wrong moment Baney would have missed the trip altogether. Yet, Charley and Clyde were sitting together on the other side of the truck and the wad of typescript was thicker.

"*Viking Columbus,*" Charley said, waving it over his head. "A wide-screen masterpiece." He handed it down and Barney saw that there were some cards clipped to the folder. "Those are our time cards, and if you examine them you'll see that they have been punched in every day, and Clyde and I are asking double time for Saturdays and treble for Sundays."

"Who's arguing?" Barney said, weighing the script happily. "Come on along, Charley, we'll have the story conference right away."

Charley sniffed the twilight air as they came out of the warehouse. "What a lot of stinks," he said. "I never realized it before. What great air we had there on the island." He looked down at his feet while he walked. "Feels funny to be wearing shoes again."

"The native's return," Barney said. "I'll bring the script in and you can get some clothes from wardrobe to replace your beachcomber's rags and grab a shave. Get over to L.M.'s office as soon as you can. Is it a good script?"

"Maybe it's too early to say—but in a way I think it's the best thing I have ever done. Working the way I did, no outside distractions you know—if you don't count the eyes! And Clyde was a big help, a good clean typist. He's a poet, did you know that?"

"I thought he was a cook?"

"He's a lousy cook, I ended up doing all the cooking. He only took the job in the commissary to pay his rent. He's a damn good poet, and great on dialogue. He helped me a lot there. Do you think we can get him a credit on this film?"

"I don't see why not. And don't forget that shave."

Barney went into L.M.'s office and dropped the script onto the desk. "Finished," he said.

L.M. weighed it carefully in both hands, then held it at arm's length so he could read the cover sheet.

"*Viking Columbus*. A good title. We'll have to change it. You delivered like you said, Barney, so maybe now you can tell me the secret of in one hour producing a script. Tell Sam, he wants to hear too." Sam was almost invisible, immobile against the dark wallpaper, until he nodded his head.

"No secret, L.M., it's the vremeatron. You saw it in action. Charley Chang went back in time to a nice quiet spot where he worked very hard to produce this script. He stayed as long as he needed, then we brought him back to almost the same moment when he left. Hardly any time at all elapsed here while he was away, so from your point of view it looks like it took just an hour to produce a complete script."

"A script in an hour!" L.M. said, beaming happily. "This is going to revolutionize the business. Don't be cheap, Barney. Give me the highest hourly rate you can imagine, then double it—twice! I don't care about money. I want to do the right thing and see that Charley Chang gets the greatest rate per hour ever paid to man, paid for one hour of his time."

"You missed the point, L.M. Maybe only an hour of *your* time went by, but Charley Chang worked more than two months on that script, Saturdays and Sundays included, and he has to get paid for that time."

"He can't prove it!" L.M. said, scowling fiercely.

"He can prove it. He punched a time clock every day and I have the time cards right here."

"He can sue! One hour it took, one hour I pay for."

"Sam," Barney pleaded, "talk to him. Tell him you don't get nothing for nothing in this world. Eight weeks' pay is still beans for a great script like this."

"I liked the one-hour script better," Sam said.

"We all liked the one-hour script better, except there never was a one-hour script. This is just a new way of working, but we still have to pay the same amount for the work whatever happens."

The buzz of the phone interrupted and L.M. picked it up, first listening, then answering with a monosyllabic series of grunts, finally slamming the handpiece back into the cradle.

"Ruf Hawk is on his way up," L.M. said. "I think maybe we can use him for the lead, but also I think he is under contract to an independent for another picture. Feel him out, Barney, before his agent gets here. Now—about this one hour . . ."

"Later we discuss the one hour, please, L.M. It'll work out."

Ruf Hawk came in, stopping for a moment in the doorway and turning his head in profile so they could see how good he looked. He looked good. He looked good because that was really the only thing in life that he cared about. While all around the world, in countless movie houses, women's hearts beat faster when they watched Ruf lock some lucky starlet in his firm embrace, little did these countless women know that their chances of getting locked in that embrace were exactly zero. Ruf did not like women. Not that he was a queer or something, he didn't like men either. Or sheep or raincoats or whips, etc. Ruf just liked Ruf, and the light of love in his eyes was nothing more than a reflected gleam of narcissistic appreciation. He had

52

been just one more slab of beefcake on muscle beach until it was discovered that he could act. He couldn't act really, but it had been also discovered that he could act what he had been told to act. He would follow exactly whatever instructions were given to him, repeating the same words and actions over and over again with infinite bovine patience. Between takes he refreshed himself by looking into a mirror. His incompetence had never been revealed, because, in the kind of pictures he appeared in, before anyone could notice how bad he was the Indians would attack or the dinosaurs stampede or the walls of Troy would get torn down or something else mildly distracting would happen. Therefore Ruf was happy, and when the producers looked at box-office receipts they were happy, and everyone agreed that he had plenty of mileage left in him before his gut began to spread.

"Hi, Ruf," Barney said, "just the man we want to see."

Ruf raised his hand in greeting and smiled. He didn't talk much when he hadn't been told to talk.

"I'm not going to beat around the point, Ruf, all I'm going to say is that we're going to make the world's greatest picture and we were talking about a lead and your name was mentioned, and I said right out loud if we are going to do a Viking picture, then Ruf Hawk is the most vikingest Viking I can think of."

Ruf showed no signs of emotion or interest at this revelation. "You've heard of Vikings, haven't you, Ruf?" Barney asked.

Ruf smiled slightly.

"You remember," Barney said, "tall guys with big axes and horns on their helmets always sailing around in ships with a carved dragon in front . . ."

"Oh, yeah, sure," Ruf said, his attention captured at last. "I've heard of Vikings. I've never played a Viking."

"But in your heart of hearts you have always wanted to play a Viking, Ruf, it couldn't be any other way. This is the kind of role that is made for you, the kind of role you can sink your teeth into, the kind of role that will make you look great in front of the camera."

The thick eyebrows slowly crawled together to form a

frown. "I always look great in front of the camera."

"Of course you do, Ruf, that's whay we have you here. You haven't got any big commitments, any other pictures, do you?"

Ruf frowned even deeper as he thought. "Got a picture coming up end of next week, something about Atlantis."

L.M. Greenspan glanced up from the script and matched his frown to Ruf's. "I thought so. My apologies to your agent, Ruf, but we gotta find someone else."

"L.M.," Barney said. "Read the script. Enjoy it. Let me talk to Ruf. You've forgotten that this film will be in the can by Monday, which will give Ruf three days to rest up before Atlantis sinks."

"I'm glad you mentioned the script because it has some grave faults, big ones."

"How can you tell—you've only read ten pages? Read it a bit more, then we'll talk about it, the writer is waiting outside right now. Any changes that are needed he can make them practically while you wait." He turned back to Ruf. "You're going to get your wish and play that Viking. We've got a new technical process whereby we go on location to shoot the picture, and, though we'll be back in only a couple of days, you get paid for a feature-length picture. What do you think of that?"

"I think you better talk to my agent. Anything to do with money I don't say a word."

"That's the way it should be, Ruf, that's what agents are for and I wouldn't have it any other way."

"It just won't do," L.M. said in a voice of doom. "From Charley Chang I expected better. The opening won't do."

"I'll get Charley in now, L.M., and we'll thrash this out, find the trouble and lick it."

Barney looked at the clock: 8:00 P.M. And get hold of this slab of muscle's agent. And fight the script through a rewrite and shoot Charley back to Catalina—and his teeth and eyes—to do the job. And find actors for the supporting roles. And get every single item lined up that they might need for a couple of months of shooting, then get the entire company moved back in time. And shoot the picture in the eleventh century, which should raise some interesting problems of its own. And get the entire thing done, finished and in the can by Monday morning. And here it was eight o'clock of a Wednesday night. Plenty of time.

Sure, nothing to it, plenty of time.

Then why was he sweating?

7

"A miracle of logistics, that's what I call it, Mr. Hendrickson, getting all this done in less than four days," Betty said, as they walked along the column of trucks and trailers that stretched along the concrete roadway leading to sound stage B.

"That's not what I would call it," Barney said, "but I'm always very careful what words I use in front of women. How does the list check out?"

"All systems go. All the departments have turned in their check lists completed and signed. They've really done wonderfully."

"Fine—but where is everybody?"

They had passed almost all the vehicles and Barney realized that, other than a few drivers, he had seen nobody.

"It was after you left last night to get the raw film, and everyone was sitting around and we couldn't leave and that sort of thing. Well, you know, one thing led to another . . ."

"No, I don't know. What sort of things led to what sort of things?"

"It was fun, really, and we did miss you. Charley Chang ordered two cases of beer from the commissary because he said he hadn't had a beer in a year, and someone else got some drinks and sandwiches, and before you knew it there was a real swinging party going. It went on very late, so I guess they must all be pooped and still asleep in the trailers."

"Are you sure? Did anyone make a head count?"

55

"The guards weren't drinking and they said no one left the area so it must be all right."

Barney looked at the row of silent trailers and shrugged. "Good enough, I guess. We'll do a roll call after we arrive and send back for anyone who is missing. Let them sleep during the trip, it's probably the best way. You better get some sleep yourself if you have been up all night."

"Thanks, bossman. I'll be in trailer twelve if you need me."

The sound of rapid hammering echoed from the gaping doors of the sound stage, where the carpenters were putting the final bit of flooring onto the time platform. Barney stopped just inside the door and lighted a cigarette and tried to work up an enthusiastic attitude toward the jerry-rigged fabrication that was to take the company on location in the Orkneys. A rectangular channel-iron frame had been welded to the professor's specifications, then floored with heavy planks. As soon as the first bit of planking was down at the front end a windowed control room had been built and Professor Hewett had mounted his enlarged vremeatron—which in addition to being larger seemed to have far more festooned wires and glittering coils than the original—and a heavy-duty diesel motor-generator. Almost two dozen large truck tires had been fastened to the bottom of the platform to absorb any landing shock, a pipe railing had been put along the sides and a rickety-looking pipe structure went across the top to delimit the edges of the time field. The whole thing looked insubstantial and shoddy and Barney decided that the best thing he could do would be not to think about it.

"Start it up," Professor Hewett said, crawling out from behind his apparatus with a smoking soldering iron in his hand. A grip bent over the diesel engine, which groaned and turned over, then coughed out a cloud of blue exhaust and broke into hammering life.

"How is it going, Prof?" Barney asked through the open door. Hewett turned and blinked at him.

"Mr. Hendrickson, good morning. I presume you are enquiring about the condition of my vremeatron mark two, and I am pleased to answer in the affirmative. It is ready to begin operation at any time, the circuits are all tested and I am ready whenever you are."

Barney looked at the carpenters, who were hammering home the last boards, then kicked a scrap of wood off the platform. "We'll leave at once—unless you've found a way to beat the return trip trouble?"

Hewett shook his head *no*. "I have experimented with the vremeatron to see if this barrier can be crossed, but it is impossible. When we return in time we cut an arc through the continuum, using energy to warp our own time lines out of the world time line. The return trip, after a visit in the past, no matter how prolonged the visit, is a reverse voyage along the same time-vector that was established by the original time motion. In a sense the return voyage may be called endotempic, an absorption of time energy, just as the outward or backward voyage was exotempic. Therefore we can no more return to a point in time before the time of our original parting from the world time line, than a dropped ball on rebound can bounce higher than its original point when first dropped. You understand?"

"Not a single word. Could you try it again—in English this time?"

Professor Hewett picked up a clean piece of pine board, licked the tip of his ball-point pen and drew a simple diagram.

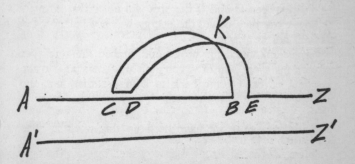

"Examine this," he said, "and all will be instantly clear. The line $A^1 Z^1$ is the world time line, with A^1 the past

57

and Z^1 the future. The point B represents our consciousness, today, our 'right now' in time. The line A Z is the time line of the vremeatron making a voyage in time, or our own time lines as we travel with it. You will note that we leave the world line at point B, today, and arc back through the extratemporal continuum to arrive at—say 1000 A.D., at point C. Therefore the arc BC is our voyage. We re-enter the world time line at C and stay for a while, moving with the world line, and the duration of our visit is represented by the line CD. Do you follow?"

"So far," Barney said, tracing the lines with his fingertip. "So keep talking while I still know what you're talking about."

"Surely. Now note the arc DE, our return voyage in time to an instant in time, perhaps just a fraction of a second after the time we orginally left, point B that is. I can control the arrival at point E until it comes just after point B—but I can never arrive before point B. The graph must always read BE, never EB."

"Why?"

"I am glad you asked that question, because that is the heart of the matter. Look again at the graph and you will note point K. This is the point where arc BC crosses arc DE. That point K must exist or it would be impossible to make the return voyage, for K is the interchange of energy point, where the scales of time are balanced. If you put point E between D and B the arcs will not cross, no matter how close they come, the energy will not balance, the trip will not be made."

Barney unknotted his brows and rubbed the sore spot between his eyes. "All of which adds up," he said, "to the fact that we can't come back to a time earlier than the time we left."

"Precisely."

"So all the time we have used up this week is gone forever?"

"Correct."

"So if we want the picture to be completed by ten o'clock Monday morning we have to go back in time and stay there until it is done."

"I could not have phrased it more succinctly myself."

"Then let's get this show on the road since it is already Saturday morning. The carpenters are finished so it's time to roll."

The first vehicle in the parade was a jeep: Tex was asleep in the front seat and Dallas in the back. Barney went over and leaned on the horn button, then found himself staring down the barrel of a long six-shooter held in Tex's quivering grip.

"I got a headache," Tex said hoarsely, "and I wish you wouldn't do that." He reluctantly slid the gun back into the holster.

"Nervy this morning, aren't we?" Barney said. "What you need is some nice fresh air. Let's go."

Tex gunned the jeep to life while Dallas stumbled over to the platform and dragged two metal ramps into place at the back. As soon as the jeep had been driven aboard he pulled the ramps in after it.

"That's all for the first trip," Barney said. "We'll find a level spot and come back for the rest. Take it away, Professor, back to the same landing site as the other trips, but eight weeks later."

Hewett mumbled to himself as he set the dials, then activated the vremeatron. The mark two was an improvement on the original model in that it compacted all the electrocution and nausea symptoms into a single quick twang of sensation—as though the passengers were harp strings plucked by a celestial finger—which was finished almost before it began. The sound stage vanished and salt spray and sharp, clear air took its place. Tex moaned softly and pulled up the zipper on his jacket.

"Over there, that meadow looks like a good spot," Barney said, pointing to a fairly level field that ran down to the beach. "Drive me over there, Tex, and Dallas stay with the professor."

The jeep ground up the rise in compound low, the popping of its exhaust sending the black-faced gulls screaming in circles over their heads.

"Looks big enough," Barney said, climbing out and kicking at a tuft of short grass. "You can drive back and tell the Prof to jump forward in time a bit and to land the platform over here, just to make sure he can find the right spot when we start bringing the company back."

Barney dropped to the ground and dug a pack of cigarettes out of his pocket, but it was empty. He crunched it up and threw it away while Tex wheeled the jeep in a circle and roared back to the platform. The ramps were still down and the jeep bounced up them again. Barney had a clear view as Dallas pulled the ramps in and the professor turned to the vremeatron.

"Hey . . ." Barney said, just as the whole thing vanished, leaving nothing but the jeep tracks and the impression of the rows of tires on which the platform rested. He hadn't intended Tex to go on with the others.

A cloud passed in front of the sun and he shivered. The gulls were settling down at the water's edge again and the only sound now was the distant rush of the surf as the small waves broke on the beach. Barney glanced at the cigarette pack, the only familiar thing in the alien landscape, and shivered again.

He never looked at his watch, but surely no more than a minute or two passed. Yet in that short time he realized only too well how Charley Chang had felt, stranded on prehistoric Catalina with the eyes and teeth, and he hoped that Jens Lyn wasn't too unhappy after his two months' stay. If his conscience had not been eroded away by years in the movie business he might have felt a twang of pity for them. As it was he just felt sorry for himself. The cloud moved away and the sun shone warmly upon him, but he was still cold. For those few minutes he felt alone and lost in a manner he had never experienced before.

The platform appeared and dropped a few inches into the meadow close by.

"About time," he shouted, the authority coming back with a rush as he stood and squared his shoulders. "Where have you been?"

"In the twentieth century—where else?" the professor said. "You have not forgotten point K already, have you? In order to come forward these few minutes in your subjective time I had to first return the time platform to the time we had left, then return here with the correct physical and temporal displacement. How long did it take—from your point of view?"

"I don't know, a few minutes I suppose."

"Very good, I should say, for a round trip of approximately two thousand years. Let us say five minutes, that would give a microscopically small figure for the error of . . ."

"All right, Prof, work it out on your own time. We want to get the company back in time and to work. Drive that jeep off and you two stay here with it. We'll start shuttling back the vehicles and I want you to move them as soon as they arrive so we can have room for the next ones. Let's roll."

This time Barney returned with the platform and never for an instant did he think about how the two men must feel who had been left behind.

The transfer went easily enough. Once the first few trips had been made the trucks and trailers moved smoothly through the doors of the sound stage and vanished into the past. The only mishap was on the third transfer when a truck overhung the platform, so that when the time trip was made two inches of exhaust pipe and half a license plate clattered to the floor. Barney picked up the piece of pipe and looked at the shining end, flat and smooth, as if it had been polished. Apparently this bit had been outside the time field and had simply stayed behind. It could happen as easily to an arm.

"I want everyone inside the vehicles during the trip, all except the professor. We can't afford accidents."

A tractor towing the motorboat trailer and the deep-freeze truck made up the last load, and Barney climbed on after them. He took one last look at the California sunshine, then signaled the professor to take it away. His watch said 11:57, just before noon on Saturday as the twentieth century winked out and the eleventh century appeared, and he took a deep, relieved breath. Now time—in the century they had left—would have a stop. As long as they stayed in this era to film the picture, no matter how long they took, no time would elapse back home. When they returned with the film it would be noon Saturday, almost two full days before the Monday deadline. For the first time the pressure tension drained away. Then he remembered that he had an entire picture to shoot, with all the problems and

61

miseries that would entail, and the pressure dropped heavily back onto his shoulders and the knot of tension returned, full strength.

A roar of sound burst over him as the tractor driver revved up his engine, and the clear air was filled with reeking exhaust. Barney got out of the way as the motorboat trailer was carefully backed off, and he looked across the meadow. The trucks and trailers were scattered about at random, though some of them had been drawn up in a circle like a wagon train getting ready for the Indians. A few figures were visible, but most of the people were still asleep. Barney wished that he were too, but he knew that he wouldn't sleep even if he tried. So he might as well get some work done.

Tex and Dallas were just settling down in the grass with cushions from the jeep when he came up. "Catch," he said, flipping a quarter toward Dallas, who grabbed it out of the air. "Toss. I want one of you to go with me to pick up Jens Lyn, the other can catch up on his beauty sleep."

"Tails you go," Dallas said, then cursed at George Washington's portrait. Tex laughed once, then settled himself down.

"You know," Dallas said, as they drove down to the beach, "I don't even know where we are."

"The Orkney Islands," Barney said, watching the gulls rocketing into the air before them, screaming insults.

"My geography was always weak."

"They're a little group of islands north of Scotland, about the same latitude as Stockholm."

"*North* of Scotland—come off it! I was stationed in Scotland during the war and the only time I ever saw the sun was through a hole in the clouds, but not often, and it was cold enough to freeze the—"

"I'm sure of it, but that was in the twentieth century. We're now in the eleventh and in the middle of something called the Little Climactic Optimum. At least that's what the Prof called it and if you want to know more ask him. The weather was—or is—warmer, that's what it adds up to."

"Hard to believe," Dallas said, looking suspiciously up at the sun as though he expected it to go out.

The house looked the same as when they had seen it last, and one of the servants was sitting by the door sharpening a knife when they drove up. He looked up startled, dropped the whetstone and ran into the house. A moment later Ottar appeared, wiping his mouth on his forearm.

"Welcome," he shouted as the jeep braked to a stop. "Very pleased see you again. Where is Jack Daniels?"

"The language lessons seem to have worked," Dallas said, "but they did nothing for his thirst."

"There's plenty to drink," Barney reassured him. "But I want to talk to Dr. Lyn first."

"He's out in back," Ottar said, then raised his voice to a bellow. *"Jens—kom hingat!"*[1]

Jens Lyn tramped sluggishly around a corner of the house carrying a crude wooden bucket. His legs were bare and he was caked in mud as high as his waist. He wore an indifferent sort of sacklike garment, very ragged and caught about the middle with a length of hide, while his beard and hair were shoulder length and almost as impressive as Ottar's. When he saw the jeep he stopped dead, his eyes widening, then shouted a harsh cry, raised the bucket over his head and ran toward them. Dallas jumped out of the jeep to face him.

"Hold it, Doc," he said. "Put the pail down before someone gets hurt."

The words or the stunt man's waiting figure penetrated Lyn's anger and he slowed to a halt, lowering the bucket. "What went wrong?" he asked loudly. "Where have you been?"

"Getting the production rolling, what else?" Barney said. "It's only been a couple of days since I dropped you, for us that is, though I realize that for you it has been two months—"

"Two months!" Jens bellowed, "it's been over a year! What went wrong?"

Barney shrugged. "I guess the Prof made a mistake. All those instruments, you know . . ."

Jens Lyn grated his teeth together so hard that the

[1] "Jens—come here!"

sound could clearly be heard across the intervening space. "A mistake . . . that's all it is to you. While I've been stranded here with these louse-ridden barbarians, taking care of their filthy animals. Five minutes after you were gone Ottar hit me in the side of the head, took all my clothes and supplies and all the whiskey."

"Why work for whiskey when it just there to take it," Ottar said with simple Viking logic.

"What's done is done," Barney said. "You've served your year here, but I'll see you don't suffer for it. Your contract is still valid and you'll get a full year's pay. That's not bad money for a couple of days' work, and you still have your sabbatical coming up and a full year's pay for that. You did your job and taught Ottar English . . ."

"His thirst did that. He was repellently drunk for almost a month and when he recovered he remembered about the English lessons. He made me teach him every day so he could get some whiskey if you ever returned."

"Ottar speak pretty good, that's right. Where's whiskey?"

"We have plenty, Ottar, just relax," Barney said, then turned back to Jens, thoughts of law suits dancing darkly in his head. "What do you say we call it even, Doc? A year's salary for teaching Ottar English and you're still working for us while we shoot the picture. I'm sure it's been an interesting experience . . ."

"Aaaarh!"

"And one you won't easily forget, plus the fact I bet you've learned a lot of Old Norse . . ."

"Far more than I ever wanted to know."

"So let's call it quits. How about it?"

Jens Lyn stood for a long moment, fists clenched, then he dropped the bucket and savagely kicked it to pieces.

"All right," he said. "Not that I have much choice. But I don't do one moment's work until I have a shower, a delousing and a change of clothes."

"Sure, Doc. We'll drive you back to the company in a few minutes, we're right around the headland . . ."

"I'll find it myself if you don't mind," he said, stamping off down the beach.

"Whiskey," Ottar said.

"Work," Barney told him. "If you're on a whiskey salary you're going to earn it. This picture starts rolling tomorrow and I want some information from you first."

"Sure. Come in house."

"Not on your life," Barney said, shying away. "I remember what happened to the last guy who did that."

8

"Stand still," Gino shouted. "All you got to do is stand still and you can't even do that."

"Need a drink," Ottar grumbled, and petulantly shook the housecarl with the matted hair who was standing in for Slithey. The man bleated and almost collapsed.

Gino swore and turned away from the viewfinder of the camera. "Barney," he pleaded, "talk to those Stone Age slobs. This is supposed to be a love scene and they're moving around like some kind of wrestling match on the hill there. They're the worse stand-ins I ever worked with."

"Just set up the shot, we'll be with you in a minute, Gino," Barney said, turning back to his stars. Ruf had his arms folded, staring vacantly into space, looking very impressive indeed in the Viking outfit and blond beard. Slithey was leaning back in her safari chair while her wig was being combed, and she looked even more impressive with about twelve cubic feet of rounded flesh rising from the low-cut top of her dress.

"I'll give it to you once more," Barney said. "You're in love and Ruf is leaving to go to battle and you may never see him again, so you are saying good-bye on the hill, passionately."

"I thought I hated him?" Slithey said.

"That was yesterday," Barney told her. "We're not shooting in sequence, I explained this to you twice already this morning. Let me do it once more, briefly, and if I might have a small amount of your attention, too, Mr.

Hawk. The picture opens when Thor, who is played by Ruf, comes with his Viking raiders to capture the farm on which you live, Slithey. You are Gudrid, the daughter of the house. In the battle all are killed by the Vikings except you, and Thor takes you as his prize. He wants you but you fight him because you hate him. But slowly he wins your heart until you fall in love with him. No sooner does this happen than he goes away on a Viking raid again and leaves you to wait for his return. That's the scene we're shooting now. He has left you, you run after him, you call to him, he turns and you come to him on the hill, right here. Is that clear . . ."

"Look," Ruf said, pointing out to sea. "Here comes a ship."

They all turned to look and, sure, enough, there was a Viking longship just clearing the headland and coming into the bay. The sail was furled, but the dragon's head on the bow rose and fell as the oarsmen on each side hauled the ship through the water.

"Tomorrow!" Barney shouted. "Lyn, where are you? Didn't you and Ottar arrange with this Finnboggi to bring his ship tomorrow?"

"They have a very loose sense of time," Lyn said.

Barney hurled his hat to the ground and ran to the camera. "What about it, Gino?" he asked. "Is there a shot here? Anything you can get?"

Gino spun the turret to the big telescopic lens and jammed his face against the eyepiece. "Looks good," he said, "a really nice shot."

"Get it then, maybe we can salvage something from this."

Ottar and the other northmen were running down the hill toward the house, nor did they stop when Barney shouted at them to keep out of the shot.

"What are they doing?" he asked, when they began to stream out, clutching weapons.

"I am sure I would not know," Lyn told him. "Perhaps it is some custom of greeting I am not familiar with."

Ottar and his men stood on the shore shouting and the men in the Viking ship shouted back.

"Get all this, Gino," Barney ordered. "If it's any good we can write it into the script."

Under the thrust of the oars the longship ran up onto the beach, the dragon prow towering above the men waiting there. Almost before the ship had stopped moving the men aboard her had grabbed up the shields that were slung along the gunwales and jumped into the water. Like the men ashore, they also waved over their heads a varied collection of short swords and axes. The two groups met.

"How does it look?" Barney asked.

"*Santa Maria!*" Gino said. "They are killing each other."

The clang of metal mingled with the hoarse cries as the men fought. No details could be made out of the turmoil by the watchers above—it was just a mass of struggling figures—until one man broke from the crowd and ran haltingly down the beach. He had been disarmed, he appeared to be wounded, and his antagonist was right behind him swinging an ax in wide circles. The chase was brief and the end was sudden. As the gap closed, the ax swooped down and the first man's head jumped from his shoulders and bounded along the beach.

"They play for keeps . . ." Barney said in a choked voice.

"I do not think that this is Finnboggi and his men," Lyn said. "I think this is a different ship that has arrived."

Barney was a man of action, but not this kind of action. The sound of battle and the sight of the beheaded corpse and blood-drenched sand had a paralytic effect on him. What could he do? This was not his kind of world, his kind of affair. This was the kind of situation Tex or Dallas could handle. Where were they?

"The radio," he said, belatedly remembering the transceiver slung over his shoulder; he thumbed it to life and hurriedly sent out a call for the stunt men.

"He's seen us, he's turning—he's coming this way," Gino shouted. "What a tremendous shot."

Instead of returning to the battle, the killer was lumbering up the slope toward them, shaking the ax and calling out hoarsely. The handful of movie people on the hill watched his approach, yet did not move. This was all so alien that they could think of themselves only as onlookers, they could not imagine themselves being involved in the murderous business taking place below. The attacking Viking lumbered closer and closer, until the black marks of the ocean spray and the perspiration stains were clearly visible on the coarse red wool of his blouse—and the red spatters of blood on his ax and arm.

He went toward Gino, breathing heavily, perhaps thinking that the camera was some kind of weapon. The cameraman stayed in position until the last possible instant—filming his enraged attacker—jumping away just as the ax came down. The blade smashed into one leg of the tripod, bending it and almost knocking the camera to the ground.

"Hey—watch out for the equipment!" Barney shouted, then regretted it instantly as the sweating, maddened Viking turned toward him.

Gino was crouched, his arm before him, with the glistening blade of a knife projecting from his fist in a very efficient manner, undoubtedly the result of his childhood training in the slums of Naples. The instant the Viking turned his attention away, Gino lunged.

The blow should have gone home but, for all his size, the Viking was as quick as a cat. He spun about and the blade slid into the slab of muscle in his side. Bellowing with sudden pain, he continued the motion, bringing up the ax so the haft caught Gino on the head, knocking him sprawling. Still shouting angrily, the man seized Gino by the hair, twisting his head down so his neck was taut and bared, at the same time raising the ax for a decaptitating blow.

The shot made a clear, hard sound and the Viking's body jerked as the bullet caught him in the chest. He turned, mouth open with voiceless pain, and Tex—they had not even been aware the jeep had driven up—steadied his hand on the steering wheel and fired the revolver twice more. Both bullets hit the Viking in the forehead and he collapsed, dead before he hit the ground.

Gino pushed the man's lifeless weight off his legs and stood up, shakily, going at once to the camera. Tex started the jeep's engine again. The others were still too stunned by the suddenness of the attack to move.

"You want me to go down there and give our extras a hand?" Tex asked, pushing fresh cartridges into his gun.

"Yes," Barney said. "We have to stop this mess before any more people are killed."

"I can't guarantee that won't happen," Tex suggested ominously, and started the jeep down the hill.

"Cut," Barney called out to the cameraman. "We can fit a lot of things into this film—but not jeeps."

Tex had jammed something into the button so that the horn blared continuously, and kept the gears in compound low so that the gear box screeched and the motor roared. At a bumpy five miles an hour he raced toward the battle.

Ottar and his men had seen the jeep often enough before to be accustomed to it, but this was not true of the invading Vikings. They saw what could only have been some sort of bellowing monster approaching, and understandably refused to stand before its charge. They scattered to right and left while Tex skidded the jeep in a tight circle at the water's edge, knocking down one of the men who hadn't moved quickly enough. Ottar and his followers rallied behind the jeep and pressed in on the divided enemy. The invaders broke and ran, clambering back into the longship and grabbing up the oars again.

This was where the engagement should have ended, and it would have if Tex had not been carried away with battle fever. Before the ship had started to move astern he ran to the front of the jeep and pulled a great length of steel cable from the drum under the front bumper. There was a loop at the end and he took this up and clambered up onto the jeep's hood, spinning it in larger and larger circles as he climbed. His rebel yell was clearly audible above the other shouts as he released the cable. Straight up the loop rose to settle neatly over the dragon's head onto the high stem post. He gave it a pull to settle it home, then leisurely jumped down and dropped into the driver's seat.

With slow grace the longship began to glide astern as the oars churned up a froth. Tex lit a cigarette and let the cable run out until twenty, thirty feet of it stretched between the ship and the jeep. One of the Vikings aboard the ship was hacking at the steel cable, with no results other than the ruination of the edge of his ax. Tex reached out his shoe and kicked the power takeoff into gear. The cable rose dripping from the water, grew taut and bar-straight, and the longship shuddered through its length and halted. Then, slowly, but steadily, it was dragged back onto the beach. The oars splashed and dug deep into the water to no avail.

It was all over then but the mopping up. Whatever enthusiasm had carried the raiders ashore had been wiped out by this last maneuver. Weapons splashed over the sides and the men raised their arms in surrender. Only one of them had any fight left, the man in the bow who had been hacking at the cable. With his ax in one hand, round shield in the other, he jumped ashore and charged the jeep. Tex cocked his revolver and waited, but Ottar joined the fight and cut off the attack. Both men shouted insults at each other as they circled warily at the water's edge. Tex carefully released the hammer and slid the gun back into its holster when he saw that all other action had stopped as the two champions joined battle.

Ottar, drenched with perspiration and already elated by the fighting, was working himself into a berserker rage, roaring and biting at the rim of his shield and running forward until the waves were up to his thighs. The invading chieftain stood scant yards away, glowering out from under the edge of his iron helmet, shouting his own guttural insults. Ottar beat the flat of his ax against his shield with thudding sledge blows—then suddenly charged, swinging his ax in a looping blow at the other's head. The invader's shield swung up to deflect the ax, but the force of the stroke was so powerful that it drove the man to his knees.

There was a note of pure joy in Ottar's bellow as he swung his ax again and again, never slowing, with the relentless measure of a woodsman felling a tree. The invader could not bring his own ax up, in fact he was leaning on his ax arm for support against the rain of blows. Pieces of wood few from the shield and a wave sent spray swirling around them.

For an instant the rhythm of ax on shield slowed as Ottar swung his weapon high and brought it straight down

70

with all his strength at the other's head. The shield went up, but could not stop it. The ax glanced from it, scarcely slowed, and hewed down into the Viking's thigh. He howled with pain and swung his own ax in a backhand blow. Ottar jumped away, dodging it easily, and paused a moment to see the effect of his stroke. The invader struggled to a standing position, with all of his weight on his good leg, and it could be seen that the other was cut halfway through and pouring out blood. At this happy sight Ottar threw away his sword and ax and gave a shout of victory. The wounded Viking tried to attack him, but he dodged away, laughing at the clumsy attempt. All the northmen on shore—and most of the men in the ship— were laughing at the wounded man's helpless anger. He kept crawling after Ottar, making feebler and feebler attempts to bring down his dancing enemy.

Ottar must have realized that this kind of fun could end only in his enemy's death by bleeding, because he ran in suddenly and hit the man on the back, pushing him face downward into the frothing water. Then, with one foot on the Viking's ax hand, he seized the man's head in both hands and ground his face down into the sand and gravel, holding it there despite the frantic writhings until his enemy perished. Drowned in the few inches of bubbling sea. All the men on the beach and in the ship cheered.

On the hill above there was only a shocked silence, broken by Ruf Hawk, who stumbled away to throw up. Barney noticed for the first time that Gino was back at the camera. "Did you get the fight?" he asked, painfully aware that his voice cracked as he said it.

"All in here," Gino said, slapping the film container. "Though from this far away I'm not sure I got all the details."

"That's all for the best," Barney said. "Let's wind up the shooting for the day, the light will be going soon and I don't think anyone wants to work with that around . . ." He nodded toward the grisly scene on the beach below.

"Doesn't bother me," Slithey said. "Reminds me of the slaughterhouse where my father worked when we lived in Chicago. I used to bring him his lunch every day."

"Not all of us have your advantage," Barney said.

"Seven-thirty tomorrow on the dot, we'll pick up where we left off today." He started down the hill toward the noisy mob scene below.

The dead and wounded from both groups had been pulled into a heap above the line of the waves, and the victors were already looting the ship of its supplies, starting with the ale. The surviving attackers had been grouped together under guard and were being harangued by Ottar, who strode back and forth before them, shouting and waving his fists for punctuation. Whatever he said seemed to do the job because, before Barney reached the foot of the hill, the northmen, invaders and defenders both, turned and started toward the house. Only one man remained behind and Ottar struck him a wicked blow on the head with his fist, stretching him on the ground, and two of the housecarls carried him off. Ottar was groping in the sea for his ax when Barney came up.

"Would you mind telling me what all that was about?" Barney said.

"Did you see how I hit the leg?" Ottar said, brandishing the retrieved ax over his head. "Hit him. *Krasc!* Leg next to off."

"Very well played, I saw it all. My congratulations. But who was he—and what were they doing here?"

"He was called Torfi. *Whiskey?*" The last was added in an exultant shout as Tex dropped the freed cable into the sand and dug a pint bottle out from under the jeep's seat.

"Whiskey," Tex said. "Not your favorite brand, but it'll do. That's a great backhand you got with that thing."

Ottar rolled his eyes with pleasure, then closed them tight as he raised the pint bottle to his lips and drained it.

"Wish I could do that," Tex said enviously.

Barney waited until the bottle was empty and Ottar had hurled it into the sea with a happy cry before he asked, "This Torfi. What was the trouble with him?"

The aftereffects of the battle—and the whiskey—hit Ottar at the same time and he sat down suddenly on the pebbles, shaking his great head. "Torfi, the son of Valbrand," he said as he got his breath back, "the son of Valthjof, the son of Orlyg came to Sviney . . . Torfi killed the men of Kropp twelve of them together. He also made the

72

killing of the Holesmen, and he was at Hellisfitar, with Illugi the Black and Sturli the Godi when eighteen cave-living people were killed there. They also burned, in his own house, Audun the son of Smidkel at Bergen." He stopped and nodded his head sagely as though he felt he had communicated vital information.

"Well?" Barney asked, puzzled. "What does all that mean?"

Ottar looked at him and frowned. "Smidkel married Thorodda, my sister."

"Of course," Barney said. "How could I have forgotten that. So this Torfi has been in trouble with your brother-in-law and this means trouble with you, and it all ends up when he tries a bit of manslaughter here. What a way to live. Who were the men with him?"

Ottar shrugged and climbed to his feet, pulling himself up on the jeep's front wheel. "Vikings, raiders. Go to raid England. They don't like Torfi now because he comes here first instead of raiding England. Now they go with me to raid England. They go in my new longship." He pointed the ax at the dragon ship and roared with laughter.

"And that one man who didn't want to join you?"

"One Haki, brother of Torfi. I make him a slave. Sell him back to his family."

"I gotta give these guys credit," Tex said. "No beating about the bush."

"You can say that again," Barney said, looking in open wonder at the Viking, who at that moment seemed a giant of a man in every way. "Climb into the jeep, Ottar, we'll drive you back to the house."

"Ottar ride the cheap," he said enthusiastically, throwing his ax and shield in, then climbing over the side.

"Not in the driver's seat," Tex told him. "That comes much later."

The supplies looted from the longship had included a dozen kegs of ale, most of which had been broached in front of the house, where a victory celebration was already in progress. There seemed to be no ill will held toward the former invaders, who mixed with the victors and matched them drink for drink. Haki, who had been tied hand and foot and flung under a bench, seemed to be the only one

73

who wasn't enjoying himself. A hubbub of welcoming shouts heralded Ottar's appearance, and he went at once to the nearest barrel that had a knocked-in head, plunging his cupped hands into the ale and drinking from them. As the shouting died away a rumbling exhaust could be heard and Barney turned to see one of the film company pickups come bouncing along the beach. It skidded to a stop in a rain of fine gravel and Dallas leaned out.

"We been trying to contact you on the radio for ten minutes, maybe more," he said.

Barney looked down at the radio and saw that all the power had been turned off. "There's nothing wrong here," he said. "I just made a mistake and switched this thing off."

"Well there's plenty wrong at the camp, that's why we've been trying to call you—"

"What! What do you mean?"

"It's Ruf Hawk. He came back all excited, wasn't looking where he was going. He tripped over a sheep, you know them dirty gray ones, they look just like rocks. Anyway he fell over it and broke his leg."

"Are you trying to tell me that—on the third day of shooting this picture—that my leading man has broken his leg?"

Dallas looked him straight in the eyes, not without a certain sympathy, and slowly nodded his head.

9

There was a crowd around the door of Ruf Hawk's trailer and Barney had to push his way through it. "Break it up," he called out. "This is no side show. Let me through."

Ruf lay on the bed, his skin grayish and beaded with sweat, still wearing the Viking costume. His right leg was wrapped below the knee with white bandages, now stained red with blood. The nurse stood by the head of the bed, uniformed and efficient.

"How is he?" Barney asked. "Is it serious?"

"About as serious as a broken leg can be," the nurse told him. "Mr. Hawk has suffered a compound fracture of his tibia, that is to say that his lower leg has been broken below the knee and the end of the bone has come through the skin."

Ruf, with his eyes closed, moaned histrionically at this description.

"That doesn't sound too bad," Barney said desperately. "You can set the bone, he'll be up and around pretty quickly . . ."

"Mr. Hendrickson," the nurse said in a frigid voice, "I am not a doctor and therefore do not give medical treatments to patients. I have administered first aid, I have placed a sterile bandage over the wound to prevent contamination and have given the patient an injection to alleviate the pain. I have done my duty. I would now like to inquire when the doctor will arrive?"

"The doctor, of course, he'll take care of this. Is my secretary here?"

"Yes, Mr. Hendrickson," she said from the doorway.

"Betty—use the pickup outside, Tex will drive you. Find Professor Hewett and tell him to take you back to the studio on the platform, and not to waste one second on the trip, he'll know what I mean. Find the company doctor and bring him here just as fast as you can."

"No doctor, take me back . . . take me back . . ." Ruf said, and groaned again.

"Get going, Betty. Fast." He turned to Ruf, smiling broadly, and patted the actor on the shoulder. "Now don't you worry your head for an instant. No cost will be spared and all the wonders of modern medicine are going to be at your service. They do great things these days, metal pins in the bones, you know, they'll have you walking as good as new . . ."

"No. I don't want to do this picture. This finishes it, I bet it says so in my contract. I want to go home."

"Relax, Ruf. Don't excite yourself, rest. Stay with him, nurse, I'll get these people out of here. Everything is going

75

to work out fine." But his words were as hollow as his smile, and he snarled as he cleared the wide-eyed spectators from the trailer and the doorway.

Less than five minutes passed before the pickup arrived, and the doctor, followed by an orderly with two cases of equipment, came inside.

"I want everyone but the nurse out of here," he said.

Barney started to protest, then shrugged. There was nothing more he could do at this moment. He went out and found Professor Hewett tinkering in the guts of his vremeatron.

"Don't disconnect it," Barney said. "I want this time platform operational twenty-four hours a day in case we need it."

"Just securing some of the wiring. I'm afraid a good deal of the circuitry was breadboarded, in the rush you know, and may not be too reliable over an extended period."

"How long did this last trip take? I mean, what time of day was it back there when you left?"

Hewett glanced at the dials. "Give or take a few microseconds, it is now 1435.52 hours, on Saturday—"

"That's after half past two in the afternoon! Where did all the time go?"

"It's not my doing, I assure you. I waited with the platform—and had a rather unsatisfactory lunch from the vending machines—until the truck came back. I understand the doctor was not on the premises and had to be found and the necessary medical equipment obtained before they could return."

Barney rubbed his midriff where the sensation of a cold lump the size of a cannonball was forming. "The completed film is due Monday morning and it is now Saturday afternoon and we've shot about three minutes of usable film and my lead is down with a broken leg. Time, we're running out of time." He looked strangely at the professor. "Time? Why not time? We have all of it we need, don't we? You could find a quiet spot, the kind you brought Charley Chang to, and that would take care of Ruf the same way."

He ran off excitedly before Hewett could answer, mak-

76

ing his way through the company encampment and into Ruf's trailer without bothering to knock. Ruf's leg was now in a splint to the hip and the doctor was taking his pulse. The doctor looked sternly at Barney.

"That door was closed for a reason," he said.

"I know, Doctor, and I'll see that no one comes through it. That's a fine-looking piece of work, there—would you mind my asking how long it is going to be on?"

"Just until I get him to the hospital—"

"That's very good, very quick!"

"Where I will take the temporary splint off and put on a plaster cast, and *that* will be on for at least twelve weeks, absolute minimum. After that the patient will be at least one month on crutches."

"Well, that doesn't sound bad—in fact it sounds good, very good. I'd like you to take good care of that patient, look after him if you would, and enjoy a bit of a holiday at the same time. We're going to find a nice quiet spot where you can both rest."

"I have no idea of what you are talking about, but what you appear to be suggesting is impossible. I have my practice and I could not possibly consider leaving it for twelve weeks—or even twelve hours. I have a very important engagement tonight and I must be going at once. Your secretary assured me that I would be home on time."

"Absolutely," Barney said with calm assurance. He had been over this ground before with Charley and he knew the way. "You'll be on time for your appointment tonight, and you'll be at work on Monday and everything will be fine, in addition to which you are going to have a holiday—all expenses paid—and three months' pay to boot. Doesn't that sound great? I'll tell you what happens—"

"No!" Ruf croaked from the bed, rousing himself enough to shake a fist weakly. "I know what you're trying to do, but the answer is no. I'm through with this picture, and I'm through with the crazy people out there. I saw what happened on the beach and I don't want any more part of it."

"Now, Ruf—"

"Don't try and talk me around, Barney, you're not

77

changing my mind. I got an out with this leg so I'm washed up with this picture, and even if I didn't have the leg we'd be through. You can't make me act."

Barney opened his mouth—he had a very nice remark that just described Ruf's acting—then with a sudden burst of unaccustomed self-control he clapped it shut again. "We'll talk about it in the morning, you get a good night's sleep," he mumbled between clamped lips, then turned and left before he said any more.

As he stood outside and closed the door of the trailer he closed the door on the picture as well, he knew that. And on his career. Ruf wasn't going to change his mind, that was certain. Few ideas ever penetrated the muscle and bone to that tiny brain, but the few that got in stuck hard. He couldn't force the overmuscled slob to go to a pre-historic island for a rest cure, and if he couldn't—there went the film.

Barney stumbled and looked up, then realized that he had walked through the camp and almost to the shore without being aware of it. He was alone, on a hillock overlooking the beach and the bay. The sun was just above the horizon, edging a bank of low-lying cloud with a golden light that reflected on the water, breaking and reforming in molten patterns as the waves rolled in. It had the wild beauty of the world empty of man and he hated it, and everything about it. There was a rock lying by his foot and he picked it up and hurled it, as though the sea were a glass mirror that he hoped to break and destroy. But he hurt his arm when he threw it and the rock fell short and only clattered on the pebbles of the shore.

There wasn't going to be a motion picture. He cursed out loud.

"What's that mean?" Ottar's voice rumbled from behind him. He spun about.

"It means get out of here you hairy-faced slob!"

Ottar shrugged and held out one big hand in which he clutched two bottles of Jack Daniels. "By my house you looked bad. Have a drink."

Barney opened his mouth to say something scathing, remembered who he was talking to, so instead said,

"Thanks," and took the opened one. A long, long drink felt good going down.

"I came here for my daily pay, one bottle, then Dallas say that from his own silver he buy Ottar one bottle because of fight today. This a big day."

"This a big day, all right. Pass the bottle. It's the last day because this film is over, gone, finished, kaput. You know what that means?"

"No," followed by a long gurgle.

"No, I guess you wouldn't, you untarnished barbaric child of nature, you. In a funny way I really envy you."

"Not a child of Nature. There was a man called Thord Horsehead, he was my father."

"I mean really envy you, because you have the world made, your world that is. A strong arm, a good thirst, a good appetite, and never a moment's doubt. Self-doubt, we live on it, and I bet you don't even know the meaning of the word."

"Self-doubt? That like *sjálfsmoro?*"[1]

"Of course you don't know it." The Viking was sitting now and Barney dropped down himself so he could reach the bottle easier. The sun had set and the sky was a deep red at the horizon, blending into gray overhead, then darkening behind them.

"We're making a film, Ottar, that's what we're doing, a motion picture. Entertainment and big business rolled into one. Money and art, they don't mix but we've been mixing them for years. I've been in this business since I wore velvet knee pants and right now, today, at the ripe young age of forty-five I am out of it. Because without this masterpiece Climactic is going to fold, and when they go down the drain I go with them. And do you know why?"

"Have a drink."

"Sure. I'll tell you why. Because in my long and checkered career I have made seventy-three pictures and each and every one of them has been instantly forgettable. If I leave Climactic I am washed up since there are a lot better directors and producers around who are going to

[1] Suicide.

get any jobs that I may want."

Ottar, looking very noble and heroic, the eyes of an eagle, smiled out across the sea and belched. Barney nodded agreement and had another drink.

"You are a wise man, Ottar. I'll tell you something I never told anyone before because I am getting drunk on your daily wage and you probably understand one word in ten that I am saying. Do you know what I am? I am mediocre. Do you have any idea what a terrible admission that is to make? If you're lousy you soon know it and you get booted out and go to work in a filling station. If you are a genius you know it and you got it made. But if you're mediocre you are never quite sure of it and you blame it on the breaks and keep doing just one more picture until you have done seventy-three pieces of cinematic crap and there is not going to be a number seventy-four. The funny part is that number seventy-four could have been a good picture, God knows it certainly would have been different. Down the drain. The picture died unborn, poor picture now in picture limbo. Dead picture, no picture . . ."

"What is this picture?"

"I told you, a work of art. Entertainment. Like your what-do-you-call-them, sagas . . ."

"I'll sing a song from a saga. I sing good."

Ottar stood, took a drink to clear his throat, and sang in a roaring voice that blended with the sound of the waves below.

Strike, strike, sword,
Thing of my heart where the worm is living!
Faces with anger my sons will bring vengeance.
Death has no fear. The voice of the Valkyrs
Brings new guests to the ale-hall of Odin.
Death comes. The table holds a banquet.
Life is done now. Laughing I die!

Ottar stood for a moment—then roared even louder, with anger. "That was Ragnar's song when King Aella murdered him and Aella died. I wish I could have slain him." He shook his fist at the unsympathetic sky.

80

Barney was having trouble with his vision, but he found that if he closed one eye he could see well enough. Ottar loomed over him, a figure from the dawn of the world, with his leather garments and flowing hair, the last light of sunset picking out red highlights on his skin. The saga was real to him, and life and art were one. The song was the battle and the battle became the song.

The idea hit Barney with startling suddenness and he gasped.

Well why not? If he hadn't been half potted, drinking on the shore of this ancient sea with a man who should have been dead for a thousand years, it would never have occurred to him. Well why not? Everything else about this business was madness, why not the final touch of insanity? He had the freedom and the power—and he was washed up in any case. Why not?

"Come with me," he said, climbing to his feet and attempting to pull the immobile form of the Viking after him.

"Why?" Ottar asked.

"To see pictures." Ottar was unimpressed. "To get more whiskey."

This was a lot better reason and they went back to camp together, Barney leaning a good deal on the other man, who seemed scarcely aware of it.

"The rushes ready?" Barney asked, poking his head into the studio trailer.

"Coming out of the drier now, Mr. Hendrickson," the technician said.

"Right. Set the screen up outside and let's see them. Show the other takes first, then put today's on."

"Whiskey?" Ottar asked and Barney said, "Sure, sit right down here and I'll get it."

There was a certain amount of difficulty in finding the right trailer in the dark, as well as unusually large numbers of items underfoot to stumble over, then the problem finding the right key for the lock. By the time Barney made his way back with the bottle a folding screen had been set up, as well as some safari chairs. He and Ottar settled themselves comfortably, with the bottle between them, the projector whirred and they watched the film in the wonderfully appropriate theater of open sky and stars.

At first Ottar had trouble seeing the projected films as picture, his untrained eye not connecting the moving patterns with reality. But he was not unacquainted with representational art, three-dimensional in wood carving and two-dimensional in paintings, and when he recognized the beach and his house he shouted with wonder.

Dinner was almost through and most of the company wandered over to look at the rushes. Even the ones who had not been present had heard all about the Viking raid by this time, and there were murmurs and gasps when the attacking ship appeared on the screen, cut through by Ottar's deep growl of rage. As the ship was beached and the fighting began there was only a horrified silence. The angle was good, the pictures sharp and clear, the detail almost unbearable to watch. Even Barney, who had been there at the time, felt the hackles rising on his neck when the blood-spattered Viking charged up the hill right into the camera, closer and closer.

Shouting a battle cry, Ottar leaped at the screen and crashed through it, rolling about in it and tearing at its fabric and metal embrace. Everyone else was shouting a good deal too, and one of the grips brought out a baby spot and plugged it in for light while Lyn managed to calm the Viking down and helping hands detached him from the ruined screen. While this was going on headlights appeared, moving through the camp, and a minute later a white ambulance with LOS ANGELES COUNTY HOSPITAL on its side pulled up in the pool of light from the spot.

"What a job finding anyone," the driver said. "You movie people sure have some big sets. I never woulda thought all this could have fitted into one sound stage."

Barney said, "What do you want?"

"Got a call. Pick up a broken leg case, party name of Hawk."

Barney looked around the silent audience until he saw his secretary. "Show these people the way to Ruf's trailer, will you, Betty? And give him my best, tell him I hope he gets well quick, that kind of thing."

Betty tried to say something, but could not find the

words. She turned away quickly, raising her handkerchief to her face, and climbed into the ambulance. The silence extended, and a number of people were having trouble meeting Barney's eye. He smiled a broad, secret smile to himself, and waved his hand cheerfully.

"On with the show," he ordered. "Get another screen up and let's see the rest of the rushes."

When the last foot of film had flicked through the projector, Barney stood in front of the screen in the glare of light, shielding his eyes against it with one hand. "I can't see who's out there—Gino are you here? And Amory?" There were sounds of assent from the crowd. "Good, let's set up for a screen test. Get some grips and some lights out here—"

"It's nighttime, Mr. Hendrickson," a voice said from the darkness.

"I'm not that blind—and I get the message. Overtime rates then, but I want to shoot that test now. As you probably all know, since rumor doth fly on pretty damn rapid wings around here, Ruf Hawk has broken his leg and is out of the shooting. Which leaves us without a male lead. Which may sound bad, but it isn't, because we don't have that much film with him in it that we'll have to scrap. But we need a new lead and that's what we're settling tonight, so I'm going to make a test on a guy you all know well, our local friend, Ottar . . ."

There were some shocked gasps, a lot of whispers and a couple of laughs. The laughs were what got to Barney.

"I issue the orders, and I'm in charge here, and I want a screen test and that is that!" He stopped to catch his breath and realized that he was in charge, more in charge than he had ever been before. A thousand years away from the front office, with no phone connections in between. No L.M. to bother him, even if L.M. hadn't been shut away with his phony heart attack, with the books under his mattress. The whole load was on his shoulders, and his alone, and the picture depended on what he did next. More than the picture, the existence of the studio depended on it and the jobs of everyone here—not to mention his own.

Normally this was the sort of situation that gave him

peptic twinges and sleepless nights, and left him wandering in a black hill of indecision. Not this time though. Something of the Viking spirit must have rubbed off, the awareness that every man is alone against the world and in luck if there is someone else there to help, but the help was not to be expected.

"We're doing that test now. Ottar looks the part, no one can argue with that. And if he has got a bit of an accent—well so did Boyer and Von Stroheim, and look what they did. Now let's see if he can act, at least as well as Ruf."

"Five bucks says he's better," someone called out.

"No takers," another voice answered, and a ripple of laughter ran across the crowd.

Just like that, they were with him, Barney could feel it. Perhaps the Viking madness was rubbing off on all of them. Whatever was causing it, they were on his side.

Barney slumped back in the chair and gave a few directions and sipped at the Jack Daniels while the lights and camera were set up. Only when the arrangements were completed did he stand and pull the bottle away from the nodding Ottar.

"Give it back," Ottar rumbled.

"In a minute. But I want you to sing me that saga about Ragnar again."

"Don't want to sing."

"Sure you do, Ottar. I've been telling everyone how great the song was and they all want to hear you sing, don't you people?"

There was a welcoming chorus of "yesses" and some cheers. Slithey swam out of the darkness and took Ottar's hand. "You'll play it for me, darling, it will be my song," she said, reciting a line from her last picture, which had been about some second-rate composer.

Ottar could not resist the personal touch. Still grumbling, but not meaning it, he stood where Barney told him to, and took the prop ax.

"Too light," he said. "Made of wood. No good at all."

He sang for them then, first in a chanting monotone, still examining the ax, then louder and with more enthusiasm as the song began to stir his emotions. With an

84

angry shout as he finished the last line and swung the ax fiercely, knocking over and almost demolishing one of the spots. The audience broke into impulsive clapping and cheers, while he strode back and forth before them accepting his due.

"That was great," Barney said. "Now we'll try just one more little business before we let you go. You see that lamp stand over there with the coat and helmet hung on it? Well that's an enemy sentry. You're going to stalk and kill him, just as you really would."

"Why?"

"Why? Ottar, what kind of question is that . . . ?" Barney knew what kind of a question it was—the kind that is very hard to answer. The *why* for an actor was easy enough, because acting was how he earned his bread. But why should Ottar do it?

"Forget that for a minute," Barney said. "Come over here and sit down a minute, have a drink, and I'll tell you a saga for a change."

"You have a saga too? Sagas are good."

In this pre-entertainment, preliteracy age the sagas were song and history, newspaper and book all rolled into one, and Barney knew it.

"That's fine," he said, and waved the camera on Ottar. "Just grab the bottle and listen to this story, the story of a great Viking, a great berserker and he was called Ottar . . ."

"Same name as me?"

"The same, and he was a famous warrior. He had a good friend whom he drank with and who fought beside him and they were the best friends in the world. But one day there was a battle and Ottar's friend was captured and tied up and taken away. But Ottar followed and he waited, hidden near the enemy camp, until nightfall. He was thirsty after the battle and he drank, but he stayed quiet and hidden."

Ottar took a quick sip from the bottle as he said this, then pressed his back against the trailer.

"Then it was dark and the time had come. He would free his friend. Stand, Ottar, he said to himself, stand and go save your friend who they will kill by morning. Stand!"

Barney hissed the last word, commandingly, and in a single lithe movement Ottar was on his feet, the bottle fallen and forgotten.

"Look, Ottar, look around this building and see the guard. Carefully—there he is!"

Ottar was part of the story now. He bent low and moved one eye slowly around the corner—then back.

"There is the guard, his back is turned. Creep up on him, Ottar, and slay him silently with your hands. Close them around his neck so that he dies without a sound. Quietly now, while his back is turned."

Ottar was out from behind the trailer, bent double and drifting as soundlessly as a shadow over the rutted ground. No one moved or uttered a word as he advanced. Barney glanced around and saw his secretary next to him, eyes fixed on the stalking Viking.

"Halfway to the guard, Ottar heard a sound. Someone was coming. He hid." Ottar vanished into a patch of darkness and Barney whispered, "Get out there, Betty. Just walk on and exit stage left." He took her arm and started her forward.

"Ottar hid, shrouded by the darkness as one of the women came by. She walked close but she did not see him. She went on. Ottar waited until it was quiet, then came forward again, closer and closer—until he could leap!"

Gino had to pan the camera rapidly as the Viking moved out and sprang, running—still in absolute silence —and hurled himself through the air onto the dummy. The helmet rolled aside and he had the steel rod of the lamp support between his fingers, bending it almost double in a single contraction of his muscles.

"Cut!" Barney said. "That was the story, Ottar, just the way you would have done it. Killed the guard and freed your friend. Very good, real good. Everyone now, let him know how much you liked that performance."

While they cheered and whistled, Ottar sat up, blinking rapidly, slow memory returning as to where he was. He looked at the twisted metal, then threw it aside, grinning.

"That was a good story," he said. "That was the way Ottar does it."

"I'll show you the rushes tomorrow," Barney said. "Let you see the moving pictures of yourself doing all these things. Meanwhile—it's been a long day. Tex—Dallas—will one of you take the jeep and drive Ottar home?"

The night air was getting cool and the crowd broke up quickly, while the grips put the spots and camera away. Barney watched the tail light of the jeep vanish over the rise, then realized that Gino was next to him, lighting a cigarette. He took one from the pack.

"What do you think?" he asked.

"I don't think," Gino shrugged. "What do I know? I'm a cameraman . . ."

"Every cameraman I ever met knows, deep inside, that he is a better director than any bum he ever worked with. What do you think?"

"Well—if you was to ask me, which you have, I would say that this guy is at least better than that slab of corn beef they carried away, and if the test looks like I think it will look—then maybe you have discovered the find of the century. The eleventh century, of course. Talk about method acting!"

Barney flipped the cigarette away into the darkness. "That," he said, "was just what I was thinking myself."

10

Barney had to raise his voice to be heard over the drumming roar of the rain on the trailer roof.

"Are you sure he knew what he was signing?" he asked, staring dubiously at the shaky X and thumbprint on the bottom of the contract.

"Absolutely," Jens Lyn said. "I read him both the English original and the Old Norse translation and he agreed with everything, then signed in front of witnesses."

"I hope he never gets hold of a good lawyer. According to this, he—the male lead—is making less than anyone else in the company, including the guy who takes care of the john-on-wheels."

"There can be no possible complaint, the terms of salary were his suggestion. One bottle of Jack Daniels a day, and a silver mark every month."

"But that's hardly enough silver to fill a tooth."

"We must not forget the relative economic position of the two different worlds," Jens said in his best classroom manner, admonitory finger raised. "The economy here is essentially one of barter and trade, with very little payment by coin. The silver mark therefore has a much greater value, which is very hard to compare to our price for mass-produced silver. It is perhaps better to look at its buying power. For a silver mark you can buy a slave. For two marks—"

"I get the point, enough already. What is more important, will he stick around to finish the picture?"

Jens shrugged.

"Oh, that's a very good answer." Barney rubbed his thumb against the aching spot in his temple and looked out of the window at the leaden skies and the falling curtains of rain. "It's been raining like that for two days now—doesn't it ever stop?"

"It is to be expected. You must not forget that, although the weather here in the tenth century is warmer than the twentieth because of the Little Climactic Optimum, we are still in the North Atlantic at approximately fifty-nine degrees north latitude, and the rainfall is—"

"Save the lecture. I have to be sure that Ottar will cooperate for the entire film—or I don't dare begin shooting. He may sail away in that new ship of his, or do whatever Vikings do. In fact—what does he do here? He's not exactly my idea of a jolly farmer."

"He is in exile for the moment. It appears he did not relish conversion to Christianity as King Olaf Tryggvessøn practices it, so after a losing battle he had to flee from Norway."

"What does he have against becoming a Christian?"

"Olaf would submit him first to the ordeal of the snake. In this the mouthpiece of a *lurhorn*, the larger brass war horn, is forced well down the throat of the victim, a poisonous snake is put in the bell of the horn, which is then sealed, and the horn is heated until the snake seeks escape down the pagan's throat."

"Very attractive. So what happened when he left Norway?"

"He was on his way to Iceland, but his ship was wrecked in a storm and he and a few of his crewmen made it ashore here. All this happened not too long before our arrival the first time."

"If he was shipwrecked—whose house is that he's living in?"

"I am sure I do not know. He and his men killed the former owner and took over."

"What a way to live—but it's good news as far as we're concerned. He's sure to stick around as long as he is well paid and drunk."

Amory Blestead came in, with a gust of wind and a splatter of rain, then had to lean against the door to close it again.

"Hang your things on the back of the door to drip," Barney said. "There's some coffee on the hot plate. How's the set coming?"

"Just about finished," Amory said, stirring sugar into his cup. "We knocked out the back wall of the house to get the cameras and lights in, covered it with plywood panels, raised the ceiling four feet. This was a lot easier than I thought. We just jacked up the beams and lifted the whole lot straight up, then the local labor cut sods and shoved them in to build the walls higher. These guys really know how to work."

"And cheap too," Barney said. "So far the budget is the only thing that has gone right with this picture." He flipped through his copy of the script, marking off scenes with a red pencil. "Can we shoot some interiors now?"

"Any time you say."

"Let's go then, into the rubber boots. What did you think of the screen test, Amory?"

"Absolutely first class. This Viking is a natural, a real find."

"Yeah," Barney said, chewing on the pencil, then flinging it down. "Let's hope so. He might be able to do a scene or two—but how will he hold up during an entire production? I wanted to shoot some simple stuff on location first, climbing in and out of boats and looking heroically into the sunset, but the weather has killed that. It's going to have to be interiors—and keep your fingers crossed."

Rain blew in around the side curtains of the jeep as they churned slowly over the hill along the mud track worn by the traffic from the camp. A cluster of vehicles was parked in the field behind Ottar's house, dominated by the thudding bulk of the generator trailer. They pulled in as close to the house as they could, then sloshed up the path. In the lee of the building were hunched most of the housecarls, dripping and unhappy, thrown out into the weather to make room for the film production. The plywood door was blocked partially open to admit the thick electric cables and Barney pushed his way in.

"Let's get some light in here," he said, shaking out of his sodden coat. "And clear that crowd away from the end of the room. I want to see this shut-bed thing."

"Watch out for the stain, it's still a little wet on the antiqued wood," Amory said, pointing to the double doors set into the wall.

"Not bad," Barney said.

Jens Lyn snorted. "Not good! I explained that in a simple house such as this one, the occupants would sleep on the sleeping ledge along the wall, that ledge over there, but they might *possibly* have a shut-bed, a small, doored chamber built into the wall. Small to retain the body heat, that is the purpose of the shut-bed." He swung open the five-foot-high doors to disclose a small room floored with a foam mattress and nylon sheets. "But this is an abomination! Nothing about it—"

"Take it easy, Doc," Barney said, looking at the shut-bed through a viewer. "We're shooting a picture, remember? You're not going to get a camera and a couple of people inside the kind of coffin you're thinking about. All right, drop the back."

Two carpenters took away the back wall of the cubicle to disclose a camera in a shed on the other side.

"Get in there, Gino," Barney ordered, "and I'll run

through the action. This is take fifty-four. Just in time, Ottar, you're about to go on stage."

The Viking stamped in, swathed in plastic raincoats and followed by the clucking makeup man, who held an umbrella over his head.

"Hello, Barney," he shouted. "I look good, not?"

He did look good. He had been soaked in a tub—the water had to be changed three times—his hair and beard had been washed, color-rinsed, dried, trimmed and combed, and Ruf's Viking outfit let out and recut for his massive frame. He was impressive, and he knew it and reveled in it.

"You're tremendous," Barney said. "So great that I want to take some more pictures of you. You'll like looking at them, won't you?"

"Good idea. I look good in picturss."

"Right. Now here's what I want you to do." Barney closed the shut-bed doors. "I'll be inside with the camera. You stand here and open the doors . . . like this . . . and when they are wide open you look down at the bed like this and smile slowly. That's all you have to do."

"That sounds like stupid idea. Better take a picture of me out here."

"I appreciate the suggestion, Ottar, but I think we'll do it my way. After all you are getting a bottle a day and a mark a month and you should do something to earn it."

"That's right—every day. Where's today bottle?"

"When you're *through* working, and we haven't started yet. So stand right here and I'll get around with the camera." He threw a raincoat over his head and sloshed out to the shed.

After many shouted instructions and false starts, Ottar seemed to understand what was expected of him and the doors were closed once more and Barney called for the camera and action. The camera pointed into the dark bedspace and whirred as the doors were flung open with great force. One of the handles came off in Ottar's hand and he threw it down.

"Hell-damn," he snarled.

Barney took a deep breath. "That's not exactly the way the scene should be played," he said. "You have to put

91

yourself into the part, Ottar. You've come home unexpectedly, you are tired. You open the doors to retire, then you look down and see Gudrid lying there asleep and you smile at her."

"Nobody named Gudrid on this island."

"Gudrid is Slithey's name in this screenplay. You know who Slithey is?"

"Sure—but she's not here now. This is pretty stupid I say, Barney."

Barney had been directing indifferent and bad actors for years, so he took this objection in his stride. "Just wait one minute and we'll try it again," he said.

There were a lot of rustling and grumbled complaints from the other side, but finally the doors swung open again, slower this time, and Ottar looked in. He was scowling fiercely into the camera, then he glanced down at the bed and his expression slowly changed. The wrinkled brow smoothed, the corners of his mouth rose into a happy smile and his eyes opened wide. He reached in.

"Cut. That was very good," Barney said, moving faster than Ottar and grabbing up the bottle of Jack Daniels from the bed. "I'll save this for you for later. Ow!"

The Viking had him by the wrist, which created a sensation not unlike being caught between the jaws of a hydraulic press, and the bottle fell from his limp fingers. Barney went back into the house rubbing his crushed wrist and wondering if, after all, he hadn't made a mistake in casting.

Slithey had arrived, and, when the rubber boots, coats and yards of plastic had been removed, she stood and shivered in bare feet and a diaphanous pink nightgown. She wore a flesh-colored body stocking, the garment was low cut and transparent, and the entire effect was devastating.

"Very authentic costuming, very," Jens Lyn said cuttingly, and left. Ottar sucked happily at the bottle and ignored everyone.

"I'm cold," Slithey said.

"Rig an electric heater with those lights over the bed," Barney ordered. "Take forty-three, Slithey, just climb into the sack and close the doors. It's warm enough in there."

92

"I don't want to catch pea-newmonia."

"With your insulation, honey, not a chance."

It was a brief scene, just a few seconds on the screen, but everything takes time when making a film, and before they were finished Ottar had worked halfway down the bottle and was singing happily to himself in one corner.

"Here we go, take fifty-five, you're on, Ottar, if you wouldn't mind putting your salary down for a while," Barney called out.

Much pacified by the whiskey, Ottar tramped over and looked at Slithey sprawled daintily in the oversized bed, covered by a Viking-Navajo blanket.

"She's tired?" Ottar asked. "Too many lights to sleep."

"Very keen of you to notice, but we're still making the film. Here's what I want you to do." Barney stood by the side of the bed. "You have just opened the doors, you look down at the girl asleep. Then, slowly, you reach your hand down and touch her hair. She awakes and does a fright take, shrinking away. You laugh and sit on the edge of the bed, and pull her toward you and kiss her. At first she struggles, pushes you away, but then hate turns to love and her arms steal around you and she kisses you too. Your hand slowly goes to her shoulder strap, make sure it's this one—the other one is glued on—and you slowly slide it over her shoulder. That's all. We cut there and the rest is left to the public's imagination and they have good imaginations. So let's run through it once first."

It was desperately hard work, since Ottar wasn't interested in the least and kept looking toward the bottle to make sure no one was touching it, and Barney was sweating as he fought to put the Viking through his wooden paces. The bottle was finally placed in the corner of the bed out of camera range, which at least kept Ottar looking in the right direction most of the time.

Barney took a long drink of chemical-tasting water and one more time stood Ottar on the lines scratched into the dirt floor.

"Here we go," he said. "We'll shoot this without sound and I'll guide you through it. And everyone else shut up, this set sounds like a mah-jongg party. Camera. Here you go, Ottar, you look down, that's it—not at the damn bottle—you reach out and touch her hair. Slithey wakes up, great, you're doing fine, sit down now—don't break the bed! Okay, now you reach out and we have the kiss."

Ottar's fingers closed around the bare flesh of Slithey's arm and his back straightened suddenly and he completely forgot about his bottle. Slithey's hormone magic worked just as well in the eleventh century as it had in the twentieth. The odor of scented female flesh rose into his nostrils and he did not need Barney's instructions to pull her close.

"Very good," Barney called out. "A passionate embrace and a kiss, but you don't like it, Slithey."

Slithey was squirming in his grip and beating his massive chest with her clenched fists. She turned her head away and said, "Easy, caveman, take it easy," then he was kissing her again.

"Great!" Barney shouted. "Writhe all over like that, Slithey, perfect. Force her down to the bed, Ottar. Now the shoulder strap."

There was the sharp sound of torn fabric.

"Hey—watch what you're doing!" Slithey called out.

"Forget it," Barney said. "We can run up a new nighty. This is great. Now you change, Slithey. Hate turns to burning love. Very good . . ."

"Look what he's doing!" Amory Blestead said.

"Cut. That's good. We'll print that. I said cut . . . Ottar, take your hand . . . Slithey—the scene is over!"

"Wow!" one of the grips said enthusiastically.

"Someone stop them!"

"Why—they seem to be enjoying it—and so am I."

There was a great ripping sound of torn cloth, cut through by Slithey's happy giggle.

"That's enough," Barney said sharply. "Just the shoulder strap, I'm afraid this has gone too far. Ottar—*not that!*"

"Yippee!" someone said, and after that there was just a long silence broken only by Ottar's steam-engine breathing.

Barney finally broke the spell of fascinated attention by walking over and slamming shut the doors. From the other side came a high-pitched, happy shriek. He turned and saw Gino bent over the camera. "What are you doing?" he shouted. "Cut!"

"Cut, sure," Gino said, straightening up slowly from behind the camera.

"Didn't you hear me say *cut* last time!"

"Cut? No, I must have been distracted."

"Do you mean . . . the camera was running all the time?"

"All the time," Gino said with a very wide smile. "I think you've got something really new here in *cinéma vérité*, Mr. Hendrickson."

Barney looked at the closed doors and fumbled out a cigarette. "You might say that. Though I don't know if we'll be able to show the uncut version anywhere out of Scandinavia."

"Dr. Masters could use it."

"I know a guy in Beverly Hills who rents out stag movies, he'd buy a print," Amory said.

There was a moment of silence as happy laughter echoed through the closed doors.

"And he even got a bottle of whiskey in there," one of the carpenters said dismally.

11

"One thing I really like about the eleventh century," Barney said, spearing a large chunk of white meat with his fork, "is the sea food. What's the reason for that, Professor? Lack of pollution or what?"

"It is probably because what you are eating is not sea food from the eleventh century."

"Don't try to sell me that. This isn't any of that frozen TV dinner stuff we brought along. Look, the clouds are breaking up, if it stays like this we can shoot the rest of the homecoming today."

The front of the mess tent was rolled up, which gave a

clear view across the fields, with a bit of ocean visible beyond. Professor Hewett pointed to it.

"The fish in the ocean here are identical with those of the twentieth century, to all practical purposes. But the trilobite on your plate is of a totally different order and era, brought back by the weekend parties from Old Catalina."

"That's what all the dripping boxes were about." He looked suspiciously at the meat on his plate. "Just a minute—this thing I'm eating—it has nothing to do with Charley Chang's eyes and teeth, does it?"

"No," the professor said. "You must remember we changed periods when it was decided that members of the company should spend two days a week in a different time, so that work here would be continuous. Santa Catalina is a perfect holiday spot, Mr. Chang verified that, but he was slightly put out by the local life. That was my mistake. I left him in the Devonian period, when amphibian life was beginning to emerge from the sea, totally harmless creatures such as the lung fish for the most part. But there were things in the water . . ."

"Eyes and teeth. We heard."

"So I considered the Cambrian a wiser choice for our weekenders. Nothing in the ocean to bother the bathers that is larger than the harmless trilobite."

"So you've used the word again. What is it?"

"An extinct arthropod. A form of life generally classed somewhere between the crustaceans and the arachnidans, some specimens of which are quite small, but the one you're eating is the largest. A sort of two-foot long, seagoing wood louse."

Barney dropped his fork and took a long swallow of coffee. "That was a delicious lunch," he said. "Now if you don't mind, could we talk about the colony in Vinland. Have you found it yet?"

"My news isn't too good."

"After the trilobite anything is good. Tell me."

"You must understand that my detailed knowledge of the period is limited. But Dr. Lyn is well versed on the history and he has all the records in the original sagas

96

about the Vinland discoveries and settlements, and I have been following his instructions. It was difficult at times to find a suitable arrival location, the coasts of Newfoundland and Nova Scotia are irregular to say the least, but we have been successful at this. The motorboat has been used extensively, so that I can assure you that the search has been carried out as thoroughly as was possible."

"What have you found?"

"Nothing."

"That's the sort of news I like to hear," Barney said, pushing his plate of french-fried trilobite farther away. "Get the Doc over here, if you don't mind. I want to hear more about this."

"It is true," Jens Lyn said in his gloomiest, North Baltic manner. "There are no Norse settlements in North America. It is most disturbing. We have searched all the possible sites from the tenth to the thirteenth century and have found nothing."

"What made you think that there was anyting to find?"

Lyn's nostrils flared. "May I remind you that, since the discovery of the Vinland Map, there has been little doubt that the Norse did explore and settle in North America. It is recorded that in 1121 Bishop Eirik Gnuppsson went on a mission to Vinland. The sagas describe the many journeys there and the settlements that were made. Only the exact location of the settlements is still in doubt, and discovering the location was the purpose of our recent explorations. In theory we had thousands of miles of coast to explore, since the authorities differ widely as to the locations of *Helluland* and *Markland* mentioned in the sagas. Gathorne-Hardy identifies the *Straumsfjord* as Long Island Sound, and places *Hóp* in the estuary of the Hudson River. But other authorities think the landings took place farther north, Storm and Babcock think favorable of Labrador and Newfoundland, and Mowat has actually pinpointed the location of *Hóp*—"

"Stop," Barney said. "I do not care about the theories. Did you or did you not just get through telling me that you had found no settlements or evidence of any kind?"

"I did, but . . ."

"Then all of the authorities are completely wrong?"

"Well . . . yes," Lyn said, sitting down and looking very unhappy.

"Don't let it bother you, Doc," Barney said, holding his cup out so the waitress could pour more coffee into it. "You can write a book about it, then you'll be the new authority. What is more important is—where do we go from here? May I remind those of you who have not read the script lately that it is titled *Viking Columbus* and is the saga of the discovery of North America and the founding of the first settlement there. So what do we do? We had planned to move the company over to the Viking settlements and shoot the last part of the picture there. But no settlements. What comes next?"

Jens Lyn chewed his knuckles a moment, then looked up. "We could go to the west coast of Norway. There are Norse settlements there, and it looks not unlike the Newfoundland coast at places."

"Do they have many Indians we can hire for the big battle scenes?" Barney asked.

"None at all."

"Then that's out. Maybe we better ask our local man." He looked around the tent and spotted Ottar working his way through a steaming heap of trilobites in the far corner. "Go over and disturb his lunch, Jens, tell him he can have seconds and thirds later."

"You want Ottar?" the Viking asked, stamping over and dropping onto the bench.

"What do you know about Vinland?" Barney said to him.

"Nothing."

"You mean you've never heard of it?"

"Sure I heard the *skald* make poems about it, and I talked to Leif Eriksson about his trip. I've never seen it, don't know anything. One year I go to Iceland then go to Vinland, get very rich."

"With what? Gold? Silver?"

"Wood," Ottar said, with contempt for anyone who did not know such an obvious thing.

"For the Greenland settlements," Jens Lyn explained. "They are always terribly short of wood of any kind, and in particular the hardwoods needed for shipbuilding. A load of hardwood delivered in Greenland would be worth a fortune."

"Well, there's your answer," Barney said, rising. "As soon as we finish shooting here we pay off Ottar and he sails to Vinland. We jump ahead in time and meet him. We film the departure, some ocean shots to do for the trip, then his arrival. They throw up a few shacks for a settlement, we pay some wampum to the local tribe to burn them down and the picture is finished."

"Good idea. Plenty wood in Vinland," Ottar said.

Jens Lyn started to protest, then shrugged. "Who am I to complain. If he is fool enough to do it, to enable you to make a picture—who am I to quibble. There is no known saga about a visit of someone named Ottar to Vinland, but since there seems to be no evidence as to the veracity of the other sagas I do not think I can complain."

"Finish lunch now," Ottar said.

Barney went out and found his secretary waiting for him with an armful of folders.

"I didn't want to bother you while you were eating," she said.

"Why not? After what I just ate my digestion will never be the same again. Do you know what tribolites are?"

"Sure. Big squiggly things that we net on Old Catalina. It's a lot of fun. You catch them at night with a flashlight then have a barbecue with beer. You should—"

"No I shouldn't. What did you want to see me about?"

"It's the time cards and the records, the weekends in particular. You see everyone here has been taking their weekend time, what would be their Saturdays and their Sundays, on Old Catalina—everyone except you, that is. You haven't had a day off in the five weeks we've been here."

"Don't suffer for me, Betty darling. I'm not going to relax until this picture is in the can. What's the problem?"

"Some of the skin divers would like to stay more than two days at a time. They have asked for four and said they will give up next weekend and work right through. My records are loused up as it is and this will wreck merry hell with them. What can I do?"

"Walk with me over to Ottar's house, I can use the exercise. We'll go along the beach." Barney thought in silence for a minute as they came down to the shore. "Here's what. Forget all the days of the week jazz and work it by number alone. Anyone who works five days in a row gets the following two off. If they want four days together then they have to work ten days straight, then have days eleven through fourteen off. Their day records will be in your books and on the time cards, since they're punching in here and in Catalina both. Since two days or four days away means only a five-minute ride on the time platform, everyone is here all the time and working every day as far as I'm concerned—and that is all that counts. You do your record-keeping like that, and I'll straighten it out with L.M. and the payroll department when we get back."

They were almost to the headland that bounded the cove near Ottar's house when the jeep bounced down the track to the beach behind them, its horn blaring steadily.

"Now what?" Barney asked. "Trouble, it has to be trouble. No one ever rushes up to give me good news." He stood, looking unhappy, while they waited for the jeep to arrive. Dallas was driving, and he braked to a stop without kicking too many rocks around.

"Some kind of ship coming into the bay," Dallas said. "They passed on the word and everyone is looking for you."

"Well you found me. What is it, more Viking raiders like the last time?"

"All I know I told," Dallas said, complacently chewing on a wooden matchstick.

"I was right about the trouble," Barney said, climbing into the jeep. "You get back to the camp, Betty, in case there is any roughhouse."

They saw the ship as soon as they came around the headland, a large vessel with a broad sail, coming in briskly before the following wind. The film company people were on the hill behind the house, staying together, but all of the locals had run down to the beach, where they were waving their arms and shouting.

"More murder," Barney said. "And there's my *paparazzo* cameraman on the spot ready to capture all the gore in technicolor. Get down there and let's see if we can stop it this time."

Gino had set his camera up on the beach where he could shoot both the welcoming committee and the arriving ship. That things were better than Barney had thought was obvious when they got closer, because all the northmen were laughing and waving, and their hands were empty of weapons. Ottar, who must have rushed there as soon as he had heard of the arrival, was knee-deep in the water, shouting loudly. As the ship neared the shore the big sail was lowered, but the vessel had enough way to beach itself, scraping up the gravel and shuddering to a halt. A tall man with an immense red beard, who had been at the steering oar, ran forward and leaped into the surf near Ottar. They shouted greetings and embraced each other strongly.

"Zoom in on the bear-hugging," Barney called out to Gino. "And I won't have to get a release or pay a cent to any of them," he muttered happily to himself as he watched the busy scene.

The film people were drifting down to the shore now that it was obvious there would be no violence. Kegs of ale were being rolled out by the housecarls. Barney walked over and joined Jens Lyn, who was watching Ottar and the newcomer smite each other on the biceps, with shouts of glee.

"What's it all about?" Barney asked.

"They are old friends and they are telling one another how glad they are to meet again."

"That's obvious enough. Who's Redbeard?"

"Ottar called him Thorhall, so it may be Thorhall Gamlisson from Iceland. He and Ottar used to go viking together and Ottar always talked about him in a very friendly manner."

"What's all the shouting about now?"

"Thorhall is saying how glad he is that Ottar wanted to buy his ship because he, Thorhall, is looking forward to going back to Norway and he can use Ottar's longship for that. He's asking now for the other half of the money."

Ottar spat out a single, loud, sharp-edged word.

"I know that one," Barney said. "We've been here long enough to pick up at least that much of the language."

The shouting was louder and was beginning to get a nasty tone to it. "Ottar is suggesting that Thorhall has evil spirits—*illar vaettir*[1]—in his head because he never bought any ship. Thorhall says that Ottar was singing in a different manner three months ago when he came and accepted hospitality and bought the ship. Ottar is sure now that Thorhall is possessed because he hasn't been off this island for over a year, and he suggests that a hole be made in Thorhall's head to let some of the bad spirits out. Thorhall now suggests that as soon as he gets his ax he'll show which head to open . . ."

Something clicked in Barney's mind and he roused himself from the spectator attitude that had possessed him while he watched the two heavyweights square off and prepare for a murderous slugging match.

"Stop!" he shouted, but they ignored him completely. He tried again in Old Norse, *"Nemit staoar!"*[2] with the same result. "Fire a couple of shots into the air," he called over to Dallas. "Break this thing up before it gets started."

Tex fired at the gravel so that the mashed bullets ricocheted, screaming out over the water. The two Vikings turned, their personal differences forgotten for the moment. Barney hurried over.

"Ottar, listen to me, I think I know what this is all about."

"I know what's it about," Ottar rumbled, clenching one sledgehammer-sized fist. "Nobody calls Ottar a—"

"It's not as bad as it sounds—just a difference of opinion." He tugged at Ottar's arm without budging him a fraction of an inch. "Doc, take Thorhall up to the house and buy him a couple of beers while I talk to Ottar."

Dallas fired a few more shots to keep the conversation going and eventually the two men were separated and Thorhall hurried off for a drink. "Could you sail to Vinland in your own ship?" Barney asked.

Ottar, still angry, had to blink and shake his head for a few seconds before he knew what Barney was talking about.

"Ship? What about my ship?" he finally said.

Barney patiently repeated the question and Ottar shook

[1] Evil spirits.
[2] Stop! (You, plural.)

102

his head in a very positive no.

"Stupid question," he said. "Longships for raiding, up rivers, along the shore. No good in big seas. For going across the ocean you must have a *knorr*. This is *knorr*."

The differences were obvious now that Barney was looking for them. Where the dragon-prowed Viking ship was long and narrow, this *knorr* was wide and stood high out of the water—and was at least a hundred feet long. It appeared a sound vessel in every aspect.

"Could you go to Vinland in this ship?" Barney asked.

"Sure," Ottar said, glancing up toward Thorhall and clenching his fists.

"Then why don't you buy it from Thorhall?"

"You too!" Ottar roared at Barney.

"Wait—hold on, just listen. If I kick in part of the money, can you afford to buy this thing?"

"Cost a lot of marks."

"Yachting is an expensive hobby. Can you buy it?"

"Could be."

"That's agreed then. If he says you bought it a couple of months ago then you must have—*don't hit me!* I'll give you the money and the Prof will take you back to Iceland to make the deal and things will be all okay."

"What you talking about?"

Barney turned to Jens Lyn, who had listened to the entire conversation. "You're following me, aren't you, Jens? We agreed this morning that Otatr was to sail to Vinland. He tells me now he needs a different ship for the job. Thorhall says he came and bought this one two months ago. So he must have done it. So let's arrange quick for him to do it—before this thing gets any more complicated. Take Dallas along for protection and explain the whole thing to Hewett. You better use the motorboat. Go with the whole bunch to Iceland—to Iceland a couple of months ago, buy the ship, arrange for it to get here today, then get right back. Shouldn't take you more than a half an hour. Pick up some marks from the cashier to buy the ship with. And don't forget to talk to Thorhall before you go and find out how much Ottar paid so you can bring the right amount."

"What you are saying is a paradox," Jens said. "I don't believe this is possible—"

"It doesn't matter what you believe. You're on salary. Just do it. I'll oil Thorhall up so he'll be in a better mood when you get back."

The jeep pulled away and Barney went to liven up the dispirited drinking party. The northmen stayed carefully in two groups, the newcomers behind their leader, and there were many black looks and very little drinking. Gino came up with a bottle he had pulled out of his lens bag.

"Like a slug of this, Barney?" he asked. "Real grappa from the old country. I can't drink the local brew."

"Your stuff is almost as bad," Barney told him. "But try Thorhall, he'll probably like it."

Gino pulled out the corncob cork and took a long drag, then held it out to Thorhall. *"Drekkit!"* he said in passable Old Norse, *"ok verio velkomnir til Orkneyja."*[3]

The red-bearded Viking accepted the hospitality, took a drink, coughed, looked closely at the bottle then drank again.

The jeep returned in less than the half an hour Barney had estimated, but there had still been enough time to get the party rolling, the ale flowing and most of the grappa finished. There was a marked pause in the joviality when Ottar strode over to them. Thorhall stood up quickly and put his back to the wall, but Ottar was beaming with pleasure. He pounded Thorhall on the shoulder and in a moment the difficulty was over, everyone relaxed and the party really got rolling.

"How did it go?" Barney asked Jens Lyn, who climbed from the jeep with much more care than Ottar had shown. In the few minutes he had been away he had grown a three-day beard and developed great black pouches under his bloodshot eyes.

"We found Thorhall easily enough," he said hoarsely, "and received an enthusiastic reception and had no difficulty purchasing the ship. But we could not leave without a celebration, it went on day and night, and it was more than two days before Ottar fell asleep at the table

[3] "Drink!" . . . "and welcome to the Orkney Islands."

and we could carry him out and bring him back. Look at him, still drinking, how does he do it?" Jens shuddered.

"Clean living and plenty of fresh air," Barney said.

The shouting and happy northern oaths were growing louder and Ottar showed no signs of weakening under the renewed partying pleasures. "It looks like our male lead and all the extras aren't going to be working today, so we might as well call a meeting and lay our plans for the filming in Vinland and aboard this ship—what did you call it?"

"A *knorr*. Nominative, *hér er knorrur,* accusative, *um knorr—*"

"Stop! Remember, I don't tell you how to make movies. I want to take a look at the *knorr,* she appears steady enough for a camera, and see how many scenes we can use it in. Then we'll have to make plans for meeting in Vinland, keeping track of the ship somehow. There's plenty of work to do. We're over the hump and on the downgrade now—if nothing else goes wrong."

A gull screamed loudly and Barney quickly reached out and knocked on the stained wood of the *knorr's* hull.

12

"I kill you, you *mannhundr,*[1] throw water in my face! Ottar shouted.

"Cut," Barney said, then walked down the deck and handed Ottar a towel. "Your line is, 'Stay away from that sail—I'll kill the first man that lays a hand on her. Full sail! I can smell land, I tell you. Don't give up hope.' Now that is what you're supposed to say. There's nothing at all about water in your speech."

"He threw the water on purpose," Ottar said angrily.

"Of course he did. You're at sea, miles from land, in the middle of a storm, the storm blows the spray into your

---

[1] An Old Norse term of insult that can be translated as "man-dog" but is closer in meaning to the German *Schweinhund.*

face. That must happen to you all the time at sea. You don't get angry every time it happens and call the ocean bad names, now do you?"

"Not at sea. On dry land in front of my house."

There was no point in explaining again about how they were making a picture, and how the picture was supposed to be real, and how the actors must think of it as being real. He had been over that ground about forty times too often. Movies meant nothing to this chunk of Viking virility. What did mean anything to him? Eating, drinking and the simpler pleasures. And pride.

"I'm surprised that you let a little thing like some water bother you," Barney said, then turned to the propman. "Give me a full bucket, will you Eddie, right in the kisser."

"Whatever you say, Mr. Hendrickson."

Eddie took a long-arm swing and hurled the contents of the bucket into the air stream from the wind machine, which blew the solid spray into Barney's face.

"Great," he said, trying to keep his jaw from shaking. "Very refreshing. I don't mind water in my face." His smile had a ghastly set to it because he was half frozen to death. The September evenings in the Orkneys were cool enough without the drenching, and now the rushing air cut through his wet clothes like a knife.

"Throw water on me!" Ottar ordered. "I'll show you about water."

"Coming up—and don't forget your lines." Barney stepped back out of camera range and the projectionist called over to him:

"Reel is almost empty on the back projection, Mr. Hendrickson."

"Rewind it then, hurry up or we'll be here all night."

The heaving, storm-tossed sea vanished from the back-projection screen and the company relaxed. The propmen, their platform next to the *knorr*, switched on the electric pump to fill their barrel with more sea water. Ottar stood alone, at the steering oar of the beached ship, and frowned angrily at the world. The big spotlights made a brilliantly lit stage of the *knorr* and the bit of beach beside it; the rest of the world was in darkness.

106

"Give me a cigarette," Barney said to his secretary, "mine are soaked."

"Ready to go now, Mr. Hendrickson," the projectionist shouted.

"Great. Positions everyone, camera." The two propmen threw their weight onto the long levers so that the bit of false decking that Ottar stood on pitched and tossed. "Action."

With jaws clamped, Ottar stared into the teeth of the gale, fighting the steering oar that a man out of sight below was trying to pull out of his hands. "Stay away from the sail!" he shouted. "By Thor I'll kill any man that touches the sail." The water sprayed over him and he laughed coldly. "I don't mind the water—I like water! Full sail—I can smell land. Keep hope!"

"Cut," Barney ordered.

"He's a great ad libber," Charley Chang said. "That wasn't quite the way I wrote it."

"We'll leave it in, Charley. Any time he gets that close I call it a bull's-eye." Barney raised his voice. "All right, that wraps it up for today. Morning call at seven-thirty so we can get the early light. Jens, Amory—I want to see you up here before you go."

They stood in the waist of the ship, near the big mast, and Barney kicked the deck with his heel.

"Can this thing really make it to North America?" he asked.

"There is no doubt of it," Jens Lyn said. "These Norse *knorr* were better ocean-going vessels—and faster ones— than the ones Columbus had, or the Spanish and British ships that sailed to the new world five hundred years later. The history of these ships is well recorded in the sagas."

"Remember, we've come to doubt some of the sagas of late?"

"There is other evidence. In 1932 a replica of one of these craft, just sixty feet long, made the westward passage along one of the routes Columbus used—and improved on Columbus' best time by over 30 per cent. There are many misconceptions about these vessels, for instance it is believed that they could only run before the wind with their large, square sail. Yet they could—they can—sail within five points of the wind. In fact, most interesting, the point of sailing is called *beita,* from which we derive the modern term of 'beating' up to windward."

"I'll take your word for it. What's that stench?"

"The cargo," Jens said, pointing to the large mounds with tight-lashed coverings that stood along the deck. "These ships do not have holds, so all the cargo is carried on deck."

"What's the cargo—Limburger cheese?"

"No, mostly food, cattle feed, ale, that sort of thing. The odor comes from the hide tarpaulins that are waterproofed with seal-oil tar and butter."

"Very ingenious." Barney pointed into the dark mouth of the open well behind the mast. "What happened to the hand pump you were going to install here? This ship has to get to Vinland or we have no picture. I want every precaution taken to make sure of that. Amory said a pump would be an improvement—so where is it?"

"Ottar refused to have it," Jens said. "He was very suspicious of it and was afraid it would break and he wouldn't know how to fix it. You can say one thing for the system they use, one man standing in the well and filling a bucket and another throwing it overboard with this wooden arm, it may be crude but it always works."

"As long as they have buckets and men, which I'm sure they'll have enough of. All right, I'll buy that. I don't want to teach Ottar his business—I just want to make sure he gets there. Where is this navigation thing you rigged, Amory?"

"It's sealed inside the hull where it can't be tampered with, and there's just a simple dial topside for the steersman to look at."

"Will it work?"

"I don't see why not. These northmen are very good navigators in their own right. Their sea passages are usually very short so they set their course and sail from a landmark astern to one ahead. They know how the ocean currents run and the habits of the sea birds so they can follow them to land. In addition to which they can estimate their latitude very closely by the height of the North Star above the horizon. Any assistance we give them should fit within the system they already use, so it can be an additional help—but one that wouldn't cause a tragedy if it failed. The most obvious aid would seem to be a simple magnetic compass, but that would be too foreign to them, and a compass is particularly difficult to use this far north where there are so many magnetic anomalies and where the difference between true north and magnetic north is so marked."

"That was what you didn't do. So what did you do?"

"Sealed a gyrocompass into the stern up against the hull here, along with a load of new long-life nicad batteries. We'll turn it on when they leave and it should run at least a month before the batteries poop out. The gyrocompass is one of the new microminiaturized, no-tumble, no-precession things developed for rockets. Then right here, set into the rail by the steersman, is the compass repeater."

Barney looked in through the thick glass covering at the white arrow clearly visible against the black dial. The dial was completely blank except for a single large white spot. "I hope this means more to Ottar than it does to me," he said.

"He likes it a great deal," Amory said. "In fact he is quite enthusiastic. Maybe if I draw a sketch it would be clearer." He took a felt-tipped pen and a notepad from his pocket and quickly made a simple drawing.

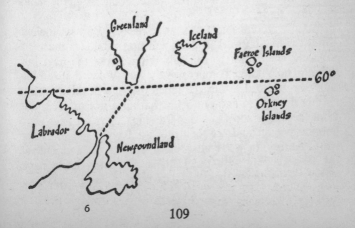

"The dotted line represents sixty degrees north latitude, and you will notice that this parallel is the one Ottar would normally sail to reach Cape Farewell here on the tip of Greenland, sailing due west and estimating the height of the North Star to keep him on the latitude. What we will do is set the gyrocompass so that it always points to Cape Farewell. When the pointer on the repeater dial touches the spot—and they both are luminescent and glow at night—the ship is headed in the right direction. They will be guided right to the tip of Greenland."

"Where they are going to spend the winter with some of Ottar's relatives. Fine so far—but what happens in the spring when they have to go on? This sixty-degree course will take them right into Hudson Bay."

"We will have to reset the compass," Amory said. "Ottar will wait for us and we'll put in new batteries and point the compass at the Straight of Belle Isle, right here. He should have enough faith in the instrument by then to follow it—even though his course won't run along a parallel. However, the East Greenland Current does flow in the same direction and he is familiar with that. He'll have no trouble reaching either the coast of Labrador or Newfoundland."

"He'll find Vinland all right," Barney said. "But how do we find him?"

"There is a radio responder sealed in with the batteries. It will automatically send back a signal when it detects our radio signal. Then it is a simple matter of our using the radio direction finder."

"Sounds foolproof. Let's hope it is." Barney looked along the low-bulwarked deck and up at the thin mast. "I wouldn't even want to sail this thing across the bay, but then I'm no Viking. Tomorrow's the day. We've done all the shooting we need to here. Launch the ship in the morning and we'll run it in and out of the harbor a few times, shoot from the shore and from aboard ship. Then turn on your homing pigeon and let them go. And your gadget better work, Amory, or we're all going to stay in Vinland and set up housekeeping with the Indians. If I can't bring back this picture with me there's just no point in going back."

110

Gino popped his head up out of the bailing well like a jack-in-the-box and waved. "They can run it up now, I'm ready."

Barney turned to Ottar, who leaned negligently on the tiller of the steer-board, and said, "Pass the word, will you."

The tired seamen grumbled darkly as they heaved once more on the windlass. They had been running the big square sail up and down and tacking about the bay since dawn, while the shiphandling sequences were being shot. As the drum of the windlass turned, the oiled walrus-hide rope creaked through the hole in the top of the mast, hauling up the dead weight of the bulky woolen sail, made even heavier by the seal-hide strips that had been sewed on to give it shape. Gino trained the camera up the mast to film it as it rose.

"The time is late," Ottar said. "If we sail today we better sail soon."

"We're just about finished," Barney told him. "I want to get a good shot of you leaving the bay, and that can be the last one."

"You shot that shot this morning, sailing into dawn you said."

"That was from the shore. Now I want to get you and Slithey at the tiller as you sail from your home into the unknown . . ."

"No woman at no tiller on my ship."

"She doesn't have to steer the thing. She'll just stand by you, maybe hold your arm, that's not much to ask."

Ottar shouted a flood of orders as the sail reached the top of the mast. The halyard that had pulled it up was secured to act as a backstay and unfastened from the drum of the windlass, then the anchor rope was attached in its place. With more heaving—caught on film by Gino—the anchor was hauled up and pulled aboard, a seaweed-hung *kilik* made from a large stone held in a framework of wooden rods. The ship was beginning to gather way as the wind filled the sail and Barney hurried the camera into position.

"Slithey," he called out. "Onstage, and make it fast."

It wasn't easy to get from the fore to the rear deck of

111

the *knorr* when she was fully loaded. Since there were no holds, and only two tiny sleeping cabins, not only was the cargo packed on deck, but in and around it were over forty people, six stunted cows and a lashed-down bull, a small flock of sheep, and two goats that stood high on the peak of the cargo. The bellowing, baaing and shouting made it hard to think. Slithey staggered her way through all of this and Barney helped her up onto the tiny deck. She was wearing a white gown with a low-cut kirtle, and looked very attractive with her long blond braids and her cheeks made rosy by the wind.

"Stand up there next to Ottar," Barney told her, then moved himself out of camera range. "Camera."

"Good shot of the back of their heads" Gino said.

"Ottar," Barney shouted, "for Thor's sake will you turn around, you're facing the wrong way."

"Facing the right way to steer," Ottar said stubbornly, holding onto the handle of the steer-board that came across the deck from the side, and facing full astern toward the vanishing land. "When leaving land always look at it, making sure of direction. That is the way it is done."

With a certain amount of pleading, cajoling—and bribery—Barney managed to get Ottar and Slithey to the far side of the handle where Ottar had to steer by looking over his shoulder. Slithey stood next to him, her hand resting on the wood next to his, and they got their shots of the receding shore.

"Cut," Barney finally ordered, and Ottar relievedly went back to the correct position.

"I put you ashore around the point," he said.

"Suits," Barney said. "I'll get on the radio and have one of the trucks waiting for us."

Slinging the camera overboard was the only tricky part, and Barney stayed aboard after the others had disembarked, waiting until it was safely ashore. "See you in Vinland," he said, putting out his hand. "Have a good trip."

"Sure," Ottar said, crushing Barney's hand in his. "You find a good spot for me. Water, grass for animals, plenty hardwood trees."

"I'll do my best," Barney said, shaking the blood back into his whitened fingers.

The Viking did not waste any time. As soon as Barney had jumped ashore he ordered, with relieved shouts and loud curses, that the *beitass* be rigged in position. This long pole fitted into a socket in the deck and the other end caught the edge of the sail so that it bellied into the wind. The ship pulled free of the land for the last time and headed for the open sea, the shouts and animal sounds fading into the distance.

"They better make it," Barney said, half aloud. "They just had better make it." He turned away abruptly and climbed into the truck. "Get me to the platform—and step on it" he told the driver. He could eliminate at least half of his fears at once by finding out if the ship would make a safe arrival in Iceland. The time machine did not simplify his problems, but it at least made the waiting and nail-chewing period a good deal shorter.

The camp was in a turmoil as they drove up, the tents being struck and everything loaded for the move to the new location, but Barney had no eyes for it; he tapped impatiently on the window frame. The entire operation was waste motion if anything happened to the ship. He was out of the car while it was still braking to a stop at the time platform. The jeep was already aboard and Tex and Jens Lyn were watching the professor charge the vremeatron batteries.

"Where's Dallas?" Barney asked.

Tex pointed with his thumb. "In the can."

"At a time like this!"

"We can go without him," Tex said. "It doesn't need the two of us for this job. All we have to do is deliver Ottar's winter ration of whiskey once we know he arrived okay."

"You'll do what I say. I want two men along for protection, just in case. I don't want any slip-ups. Here he comes now—get going."

Barney stepped away from the time platform as the professor activated the field. As always—from the observer's point of view—the voyage seemed to take no more than a fraction of a second. The platform vanished and reappeared again a few feet farther away.

It had changed though. Professor Hewett was sealed into his instrumentation shack, while the rest were in the jeep, which had its top up and side curtains attached. Almost a foot of snow blanketed everything, and a flurry of airborne snow blew out of the vremeatron's field and coated the grass around it.

"Well?" Barney shouted. "What happened? Come out of there and report."

Dallas climbed down from the jeep and trudged over through the snow. "That Iceland," he said. "What a climate they got there in October."

"Save the weather report. Are Ottar and the ship all right?"

"Everything's fine. The ship is up on the shore for the winter, and when we left Ottar and his uncle were getting smashed on the booze we brought. For a while there we worried he would never show, the Prof had to make four jumps to find him. Seems he stopped for some time in the Faeroes. Between you and me I don't think he would ever have got to Iceland if his thirst hadn't got the better of him. Once you get hooked on the distilled stuff, the homebrew doesn't seem so hot."

Barney relaxed, for the first time in a long time he realized, as the tension faded. He even managed a slight smile.

"Good. Now let's get the company moved while we still have some daylight at this end." He climbed aboard the time platform, walking carefully in the jeep's tracks so he wouldn't get his shoes full of melting snow, and opened the door of the control room.

"Got enough juice for another jump?" he asked.

"With the motor-generator going the batteries are charged at all times, a great improvement."

"Then take us ahead in time to next spring, the year 1005, and land us at a good spot in Newfoundland, one of the sites you and Lyn searched when you were looking for the Viking settlements."

"I know just the place," Professor Hewett said, leafing through a notebook. "An ideal location." He set up the coordinates on the board and activated the vremeatron.

There was the now familiar sensation of temporal

displacement and the time platform settled onto a rocky shore. Waves broke, almost over them, and a smother of spray hissed down into the snow. A dark cliff loomed above, crumbling and sinister.

"What do you call this?" Barney shouted above the boom of the breaking waves.

"Wrong coordinates," the professor called back. "A slight mistake. This is a different site."

"You had to tell me! Let's go before we wash out to sea."

The second time jump brought them to a grassy meadow that overlooked a small bay. Tall trees marched up the bowl of the hills around them in solid ranks, and down through the meadow to the sea there twisted a clear and swift-running brook.

"This is more like it," Barney said as the others climbed out of the jeep. "Where are we, Jens?"

Jens Lyn looked around, sniffed the air and smiled. "I remember this well, one of the first sites we checked. This is Epaves Bay, really an arm of Sacred Bay on the northernmost tip of Newfoundland. That is the Strait of Belle Isle out there. The reason we investigated this site—"

"Great. Looks like just what we want. And isn't the gadget in Ottar's ship zeroed in on this strait?"

"That is correct."

"Then this is the spot for us." Barney bent and picked up a handful of waterlogged snow from the platform and began forming it into a ball. "We'll leave the area down by the mouth of the stream there for Ottar. Then set our camp up over there to the right, at the top of the meadow. It looks flat enough to keep the twentieth century off camera. Let's go. Back to move camp. And I want this slush shoveled off first so we don't have anyone breaking a leg."

Dallas bent over to fasten the lace on his boot and the target was too broad to resist. Barney hurled his snowball square into the middle of the taut denim.

"Here we go, Vikings," he said happily. "Let's go settle Vinland."

13

All the world was gray, silent, damp, pressing in on them. The fog muffled everything, soaking up sound as well as sight so that the ocean before them was an unseen presence until a low wave appeared, breaking silently into froth as it rushed up the slope of the sandy beach almost to their feet. The truck, no more than ten feet away, was only a dark shape in the mist.

"Give it another try," Barney said, squinting into the damp wall of blankness.

Dallas, protected from the weather by an immense black poncho and wide-brimmed Stetson, raised the carbon dioxide pressure flask with the foghorn attached and opened the valve. The moaning blare of sound throbbed out across the water, still echoing in their ears after the valve was closed.

"Did you hear that?" Barney asked.

Dallas cocked his head and listened. "Nothing, just the waves."

"I swear I heard splashing, like someone rowing. Give it another blast, and keep it up, every minute, and listen closely in between."

The foghorn sounded again as Barney trudged up the slope to the canvas-shrouded army truck and looked into the back. "Any change?" he asked.

Amory Blestead shook his head no without turning away from the radio receiver. He had earphones clamped to his head and was slowly turning the knob of the directional loop antenna on top of the set. It rotated in one direction, then in the other, and Amory looked up and tapped the pointer on the base of the loop.

"As far as I can tell the ship hasn't moved," he said. "The bearing is still the same. They're probably waiting for the fog to lift."

"How far away are they?"

"Barney, be reasonable. I've told you a hundred times I can tell direction but not range with this setup. I can't read anything from the signal strength of the responder, could be a mile, could be fifty. The volume has picked up since we first heard it three days ago, so they're nearer, but that's all I know. And I can't work out the distance from the bearings because there are too many variables. We've been cutting back and forth so I can't use the truck's speedometer to get a baseline, and the Viking ship must have moved—"

"You've convinced me. That's what you can't tell me—but what *can* you tell me?"

"The same as before. The ship sailed from Greenland eighteen days ago. I aligned the gyrocompass with the Strait of Belle Isle, put in new batteries and turned on the responder and tested it, and we watched them leave."

"You and Lyn told me the crossing would take only four days," Barney said, worrying a hangnail with his teeth.

"We said it *might* take only four days, but if the weather got bad, the winds changed or anything like that, it could take a lot longer. And it has. But we have picked up a signal from the responder, which means they've made the crossing safely."

"That was two days ago—what have you done for me lately?"

"Speaking as an old friend, Barney, this time traveling is doing absolutely nothing for your nerves. We're supposed to be making a film, remember? All this other stuff we do is above and beyond the call of duty—not that anyone is complaining. But off with the pressure and make it easier on all of us, as well as yourself."

"You're right, you're right," Barney said, which was about as close as he could ever come to an apology. "But two days—the waiting gets to you after a while."

"There's really nothing to worry about. With this fog and no wind to speak of, laying off an unknown coast— they're not going to do any moving about. There's no point in rowing around if you don't know where you're going. Right now, according to the direction finder, we are as

117

close to them as we can get on dry land and when the fog lifts we can guide them in—"

"Hey!" Dallas shouted from the beach, "I hear something, out there in the water."

Barney skittered and half slid down the slope to the beach. Dallas had his hand cupped to his ear, listening intently.

"Quiet," he said, "and see if you can hear it. Out there in the fog. I swear I heard water splashing, like rowing, and voices talking."

A wave broke and receded, and for a moment there was a hushed silence—and the slapping of oars could be plainly heard.

"You're right!" Barney shouted, then raised his voice even louder. "Over here—this way!"

Dallas shouted too, the foghorn forgotten for the moment as a dark shape loomed out of the fog over the sea.

"It's the boat," Dallas said, "the one they had slung on deck."

They called and waved as a sudden rift opened in the mist, giving them a clear view of the craft and its occupants.

The boat was made of some kind of dark skins and the three men in it were wearing fur parkas with the hoods thrown back, uncovering their long black hair.

"They're not Vikings," Tex said, waving his arm so that his black poncho flapped. "Who are they?"

When he did this the two men in the rear dug their round paddles into the water, but the man who was kneeling in the front whipped his arm forward and something flashed through the air towards Dallas.

"They got me!" Dallas shouted and fell over on his back with a spear sticking up out of his chest. The foghorn hit the beach next to him and the valve opened and the sound blared, roaring out across the water. When it did the men in the boat reversed their paddling with vigor and within a few strokes had vanished again into the fog.

Only a few seconds had passed from the time they appeared until the instant they vanished, and Barney stood, stunned by the impact, deafened by the wave of sound. It made thinking difficult and he had to stop it before he turned to Dallas, who still lay, unmoving, on his back, looking as dead as a kipper.

"Pull this thing out, will you?" Dallas said in a calm voice.

"I'll hurt you—kill you—I can't . . ."

"It's not as bad as it looks. But make sure you pull up and don't push down."

Barney gingerly tugged on the wooden handle of the spear and it came up easily enough, but it caught in Dallas's clothing so that he finally had to brace his feet and pull hard with both hands. It came free and tore a great strip of rubberized cloth from the poncho. Dallas sat up and lifted the poncho and ripped open his jacket and shirt.

"Look at that," he said, pointing to a red scratch on his ribs. "Another couple of inches to the right and it would have ventilated me. That hook was digging into me when I moved and felt a lot worse than it looks now, let me tell you." He touched the sharp barb that projected from the ivory head of the spear.

"What happened?" Amory called out, running down the slope from the truck. "What's that? Wasn't there a boat?"

Dallas stood and tucked his shirt back in. "We have been contacted by the locals," he said. "Looks like the Indians or the Eskimos or somebody got here before the Vikings."

"Are you hurt bad?"

"Not fatal. This spearhead didn't have my name on it." He chuckled and looked closely at the weapon. "Nice job of carving and good balance."

"I don't like this," Barney said, groping out a damp cigarette. "Didn't I have enough trouble as it was? I just hope they don't find the Viking ship."

"I hope they do," Dallas said with relish. "I don't think they would give Ottar much trouble."

"What I wanted to tell you," Amory said, "from up there in the truck you can see the fog breaking up, and the sun coming through in patches."

"And about time," Barney said, dragging deeply on the cigarette so that it fizzled and crackled.

Once the sun began burning away the mist it cleared

quickly, helped by the west wind that blew steadily in their faces. Within a half hour it had lifted completely and there, clearly visible about a mile offshore, was Ottar's *knorr*.

Barney almost smiled. "Give them a blast on that thing," he said. "Once they look this way they'll see the truck."

Dallas kept triggering the CO_2 cylinder until it finally squawked and died, and it had the desired effect. They could see the big sail narrow, then widen again as it was pushed around, and the white bone of foam appeared at the bow as the ship gathered way. There was no sign of the skin boat, which seemed to have vanished as suddenly as it had appeared.

A few yards offshore the *knorr* turned and hove to, sail flapping, rocking in the gentle swell. There was a great deal of arm waving and incomprehensible shouting.

"Come on," Barney shouted. "Come ashore. Why don't you beach that thing?"

"They must have their reasons," Amory said. "The kind of shore here or something."

"Well how do they expect me go get out there?"

"Swim maybe," Dallas suggested.

"Bright boy. Maybe you ought to dog-paddle over and give them a message."

"Look," Amory pointed, "they've got a second boat aboard." The *knorr's* own boat, a twenty-foot-long miniature of the mother ship, was still visible on deck, but a smaller boat was being dropped over the side.

"Something familiar about that thing," Dallas said.

Barney squinted at it. "You're dead right. It looks just like the one the redskins had."

Two men climbed into the bobbing craft and began to row toward the shore. Ottar was in the bow, waving his paddle at them, and a few moments later he and his companions beached the skin boat and splashed ashore.

"Welcome to Vinland," Barney said. "How was the trip?"

"Coast here no good, no grass for the animals, trees no good," Ottar said. "Did you find a good place?"

"The best, down the coast a few miles, just what you

120

asked for. Any trouble on the crossing from Greenland?"

"Wind the wrong way, very slow. Plenty of floating ice and seal and we saw two *skraelling*.[1] They were killing sea's and tried to row away but we went after them, and when they threw spears we killed them. Ate their seals. Took their boat."

"I know what you mean, we just met some of their relatives."

"Where's this good place you found?"

"Right down the coast, around the headland and past the islands—you can't miss it. Here, take Amory back in the ship with you, he'll show you the place."

"Not me," Amory said, raising his hands and backing away. "I just look at boats and I get green. My stomach would be turned inside out and I'd be dead three minutes after I left the shore."

With the regular soldier's innate capacity to avoid an unpleasant task, Dallas was already on his way up the slope when Barney turned toward him. "I'm a truck driver," Dallas said. "I'll be waiting in the cab."

"All employees, loyal and true," Barney said coldly. "I get the message, boys, don't repeat it. All right, Amory, tell the truck driver to get to the camp. We'll come in the ship as fast as we can and get Ottar's people ashore, and maybe someday soon we can start making a movie again. Wake up Gino and tell him to get up on the hill, that spot we picked out, and shoot the ship when it comes in. And make sure those tire tracks along the beach are smoothed over."

"Right, Barney, just as you say. I wish I could go in your place, but me and ships . . ."

"Yes, sure. Get going."

Barney got soaked getting into the boat, and the water was so cold it felt as though his legs had been amputated below the knees. The boat, just seal skins stretched over a bent-wood frame, was wobbly and skittered over the water like a great bug and he had to squat in the bottom and hold onto the sides for support. When they reached the

[1] Barbarians. Specially used about the natives of Greenland and North America.

knorr he couldn't get out of the lurching craft and over the high side of the ship until strong hands reached down and hauled him up like a sack of grain.

"Hananú Soustu handartökin,"[2] Ottar roared, and his men shouted back happily as they ran to swing the ship about for the last leg of her voyage. Barney retreated to the aft deck so he wouldn't be trampled in the rush of activity. The seamen were shifting the *beitass* pole and the women screamed as they scattered out of the way, while the tethered sheep could only protest noisily when they were kicked aside. The crowded deck area resembled a seething farmyard, with the torn-open bundles of fodder and frightened livestock. In the middle of all the hubbub one of the women was hunkered over milking a cow into a wooden bucket. When the ship turned, the wind carried the odor of the bilges to Barney and the barnyard resemblance was even more apparent.

Once they were under way things settled down and even the animals returned quietly to their feed. The following wind not only filled the sail but it drove most of the odors ahead of the ship and the air on the rear deck was fresh and clear. The cutwater at the bow hissed through the long Atlantic swells, churning up a rounded, foaming bow wave that rushed along the sides of the ship. Riding light as a cork over the sea, the *knorr* was a graceful and practical vessel, at home in her true element.

"Land looks good," Ottar said, steering with a light touch on the tiller bar, as he pointed with his free hand toward the shore, where large trees and patches of meadow were beginning to appear.

"Wait until you get around the point," Barney told him, "it's even better there."

They were passing the islands that stood outside the bay and the animals caught the scent of the fresh grass and set up a clamor. The bull, hobbled and tied, pulled at its rope and bellowed and the women were shouting with joy while the men were singing. The voyage was coming to an end and the landfall was a good one. Even Barney felt the excitement as Epaves Bay opened up before them, with the

[2] "Come on! The last bit of work."

tall trees rising up the hills to the blueness of the skies, and the fresh spring green of the grass meadows by the stream. Then he picked out the dark spot of his cameraman and the jeep on the slope and he remembered the film. He knelt behind the bulwark and stayed low and out of sight as he pulled himself over to a horned Viking helmet that was tied by a thong to a hole in one of the timbers. Only when this was settled clammily on his head did he raise up high enough to be seen from shore.

Ottar was driving the ship at full speed toward the mouth of the stream and all aboard were shouting with excitement. The *knorr* scraped the sandy bottom, was lifted clear by a wave and carried forward, then touched bottom again and shuddered to a halt. Without bothering to lower sail, the crew and passengers were leaping into the surf and wading ashore, laughing with joy, splashing through the stream and into the meadow beyond. Ottar tore up a great handful of the knee-high grass, smelt it, then chewed a bit of it. Some of the others were rolling on the ground, taking an animal pleasure in the solid earth after all the days aboard the ship.

"Great!" Barney shouted, "absolutely great. The landing in Vinland after months at sea, the first settlers in the new world. A great shot, a great historical shot." He made his way through the frenzied animals to the bow and stood up where he could be seen by the cameraman and waved his arm in a come-on motion. "That's enough of that," he shouted. "Get down here."

His voice couldn't carry but the gesture was unmistakable. Gino stood up from behind the camera and waved back, then began to load the camera into the jeep. A few minutes later it churned along the beach and Barney jumped down from the ship and ran to meet it.

"Hold it," he called to Dallas, who was driving. "Swing around and get up on that bank there, directly opposite the stream. Gino, set the camera up on the top so we can get a head-on shot of the ship coming in, people running off, right into the camera, streaming by on both sides."

"Absolutely a tremendous picture," Gino said, "the way they came out of the ship. Give me ten minutes."

"You got it. It'll take longer than that to set the shot up
123

again. Hold it," he ordered Dallas, who was starting to swing the jeep around. "I want your bottle."

"What bottle?" Dallas asked, with open and innocent eyes.

"The bottle you always got with you, come on. A loan, you'll get it back later."

The stunt man reluctantly produced a black-labeled, one-quarter-empty bottle of whiskey from under the seat.

"Well, well," Barney said coldly. "Been getting into the private stock."

"I ran out, an accident, I'll pay it back."

"And I thought I had the only key to this stuff. The things the Army taught people! Get moving." He stuck the bottle inside his jacket and walked back to Ottar, who was kneeling by the stream and snuffling up water from his cupped hands.

"Get them back aboard, will you," Barney said. "We want to shoot the landing again, from much closer up."

Ottar looked up and blinked, wiping the water from his flowing beard with the back of his hand. "What you talk about, Barney? Everyone happy to be on land. They won't go back onto the ship."

"They will if you tell them to."

"Why should I tell them to? A nuts idea."

"You tell them to because you're back on the job. Here's some salary." He passed the bottle to Ottar, who smiled broadly and raised it to his lips. Barney finished convincing him while he drank.

It wasn't easy to get them back aboard, even for Ottar. He finally lost his temper, something he did readily, stretched one man on the sand with a blow to the chest and kicked two of the women in the right direction. After this, though there was much grumbling and shouting complaints, they pulled themselves aboard and unshipped the oars. The effort of dragging the *knorr* free quieted the rest of the rebellion.

Onshore, as soon as the camera was unloaded, Barney sent the jeep racing back to the camp. It had returned, before the ship had reversed in the bay and raised its sail again, with the rear seat filled with cases of beer, boxes of cheese, and canned hams.

"Dump it out," Barney ordered, "about ten yards beyond the camera, and build it up high so they can see it. Break out the hams so they will know what they are. Bring me a ham and a can of beer."

"Here they come," Gino said. "Tremendous, absolutely fantastic."

At full tilt the *knorr* raced across the bay, until the big square sail loomed up above them, driving into the mouth of the stream with a great splashing of spray. Barney wasn't sure if the enthusiasm would carry through this second landing and he wasn't taking any chances.

"Ol!" he shouted at the top of his lungs. *"Svínakjöt, öl ok ostr!"*[3]

They got the message. After almost three weeks on a cold ration of hard bread and dried fish they roared with enthusiasm. The reaction this time was as good—or better—than the first arrival. They fought to get ashore, trampling each other into the shallows, and raced by the camera to get at the food and drink.

"Cut." Barney said, "but don't go away. As soon as they stoke up I want to get them unloading the wildstock." Ottar came up, a half-consumed ham in one fist and the bottle in the other. "Do you think this will do for your camp?" Barney asked.

Ottar looked around and nodded happily. "Good grass, good water. Plenty of wood on the shore for burning. Plenty of trees with hard wood over there for cutting. Fish, hunt, this is a good place. Where's Gudrid? Where's everybody?"

"Taking a day off," Barney told him, "back on Old Catalina. A day off with pay, big party, barbecue, the works."

"Why party?"

"Because I'm generous and like to see people happy and we couldn't do anything until you arrived, and because it saves money. I've been waiting here for you with a skeleton staff for three weeks. Everyone else at the party will be gone only one day."

"Want to see Gudrid."

[3] "Ale!" . . . "Pork, ale and cheese!"

125

"Slithey you mean. And I imagine she wants to see you too."

"Been a long time."

"You're a man of simple pleasures, Ottar. At least finish your ham first and remember that this is a historical moment. You have just arrived in the New World."

"You nuts, Barney. Same old world, just a place name of Vinland. Looks like good trees here."

"I'll remember those historical words," Barney said.

14

"I don't feel so good this morning," Slithey said, loosening the large gilt buckle on her belt. "It must be the air here or the climate or something."

"Something like that," Barney said with complete lack of sympathy. "The air. Of course it couldn't be that Viking barbecue on the beach last night with roasted clams and blue mussels over a driftwood fire and six cases of beer gone through."

She didn't answer him, but there was a deepening of the green tinge to her peaches and cream skin. He shook another two pills into the rattling handful he already had and held them out to her.

"Here, take these, and I'll get you a glass of water."

"So many," she said weakly. "I don't think I can get them down."

"You better, we have a day's shooting ahead of us. This is Dr. Hendrickson's guaranteed morning-after and hangover cure. Aspirin for the headache, Dramamine for the nausea, bicarbonate for the heartburn, Benzedrine for the depression and two glasses of water for the dehydration. It never fails."

While Slithey was choking over the pills Barney's secretary knocked on the trailer door and he shouted for her to come in.

"You look very bright-eyed and bushy-tailed this morning," he said.

"I'm allergic to mussels so I went to bed early." She held up the day's call sheet. "I've got a query for you." She ran her finger down the list. "Artists, okay . . . stand-ins, okay . . . camera department, okay . . . props. They want to know if you want blood with the collapsible dagger?"

"Of course I do—we're not shooting this film for the kiddy matinée." He stood and pulled his jacket on. "Let's go, Slithey."

"I'll be with you in a moment," she said in a faint voice.

"Ten minutes, no more, you're in the first scene."

It was a clear day and the sun had already cleared the ridge behind them and was casting long shadows from the sod huts and birch-bark-roofed lean-tos in the meadow below. The Norse settlers were already busy and a thread of blue smoke rose straight up from the hole in the ridge of the largest building.

"I hope Ottar is in better shape than his leading lady," Barney said, squinting across the water of the bay. "Are those rocks there, just to the left of the island, Betty—or is it a boat?"

"I don't have my glasses with me."

"It could be the motorboat—see it's closer. And it's about time they decided to come back."

Betty had to run to keep up with his long strides down the slope toward the shore, skirting a huddle of cud-chewing cows. The boat was clearly visible now and they could hear the faint pop-pop of its motor across the water. Most of the company was waiting on the shore near the *knorr* and Gino was setting up the camera.

"Looks like the explorers are coming home," he called out to Barney, and pointed at the boat.

"I can see them and I can take care of it myself, so everyone else can stay on camera. We're going to shoot this scene as soon as I've talked to them."

Barney waited, almost at the water's edge as the boat came in. Tex was in the stern steering the outboard and Jens Lyn sat in front of him. Both men had good growths of beard and a decidedly scruffy look.

"Well?" Barney asked, even before the boat touched shore. "What news?"

Lyn shook his head with unconcealed Scandinavian gloom. "Nothing," he said, "anywhere along the coast. We went as far as we could with the gasoline we had, but found no one."

"Impossible. I saw those Indians with my own eyes—and Ottar killed a couple more. They have to be around somewhere."

Jens climbed ashore and stretched. "I would like to find them as much as you would. This is a unique opportunity for research. The construction of their boats and the carving of the spear leads me to suspect that they are members of the almost unknown Cape Dorset culture. We know comparatively little about these people, just some facts gleaned from digging on archeological sites, and a few hints from the sagas. As far as we can ascertain the last of them seem to have vanished about the end of this century, the eleventh century . . ."

"I'm not interested in your unique opportunity for research but in my unique opportunity to finish this picture. We need Indians in it—where are they? You must have seen some signs of them?"

"We did discover some camps on the shore, but they were deserted. The Cape Dorset are a migratory people, following the seal herds for the most part, and the schools of cod. I feel that, at this time of year, they may have moved farther north."

Tex heaved the motorboat's bow up on the beach, then sat down on it. "I don't want to tell the Doc here his business, but well . . ."

"Superstition!" Lyn snorted. Tex cleared his throat and spat into the water. This was obviously a difference of opinion they had had before.

"What is it? Out with it," Barney ordered.

Tex scratched the dark stubble on his jaw and spoke, not without reluctance.

"Look, the Doc is right. We didn't see anything or anybody except some old campsites and piles of seal bones. But, well, I think they're out there somewhere, close by, and they been watching us all the time. It wouldn't be hard to do. You can hear this lawnmower engine five miles away. If they're seal hunters, like the Doc says, they could lay low when they heard us coming and we'd never see a thing. I think they're out there."

"Do you have any evidence to support this theory?" Barney asked.

Tex writhed unhappily and scowled. "I don't want to hear no laughing or anything," he said pugnaciously.

Barney remembered his record as an instructor in unarmed combat. "One thing I'm never going to do, Tex, is laugh at you," he said sincerely.

"Well . . . it's like this. We used to feel it in the jungle, like someone was looking at you. Half the time someone was. Bang, a sniper. I know the feeling. And I been getting it all the time we been out. They're out there, somewhere close, so help me they are."

Barney considered the information, and cracked his knuckles. "Yes, I suppose you're right, but I don't see how it's going to help us. We'll talk about it during lunch, see if we can figure something out. We need those Indians."

Nothing went right with the scene, which was probably Barney's fault. His mind wasn't on it. It should have been simple enough to shoot, since it was mostly action. Orlyg, played by Val de Carlo, is Thor's best friend and right-hand man, but he has secretly fallen in love with Gudrid, who is afraid to tell Thor because of the trouble it will cause. His passion becomes too great however, and, since Gudrid has told him she can love no other man while Thor is alive, he resolves in a moment of love-inflamed madness to slay Thor. He hides behind the ship and attacks Thor when he passes. Thor at first cannot believe it, however he does believe it when Orlyg stabs him in the arm. Then, with only one arm and barehanded, Thor goes on to win the battle and kill Orlyg.

"All right," Barney called out, his temper worn thin. "We're going to try it again and this time I'd be very obliged if you could manage to get it right and remember your lines and everything, because we're running out of blood and clean shirts. Positions. Orlyg, behind the boat, Thor start down the beach toward him, camera, action."

Ottar stamped heavily through the sand and managed to look faintly surprised when de Carlo jumped out at him.

"Ho, Orlyg," he said woodenly. "What are you doing here, what does this mean . . . *mikli Ooinn!*[1] Look at that!"

"Cut!" Barney shouted. "That's not your line, you know better than that . . ." He shut up abruptly as he looked out into the bay where Ottar was pointing.

One after another, small, dark boats were coming into sight from behind the island and soundlessly paddling toward the shore.

"Axir, sverol!"[2] Ottar ordered, and looked around for a weapon.

"Hold it," Barney ordered. "No weapons and no fighting. We want to keep this friendly if we can, find something to trade with them. Those are potential extras out there and I don't want them frightened off. Tex, keep your gun handy—but out of sight. If they start any trouble you finish it . . ."

"A pleasure."

"But don't start any yourself, and that's an order. Gino, are you catching them?"

"In the bag. If you'll clear the twentieth-century types off the set I'll shoot the whole arrival, the landing, the works."

"You heard him, move. Off camera. Lyn—get into Viking rig quick so you can get down there and translate."

"How can I? Not a single word of their language is known."

"You'll pick it up. You're translator—so translate. We need a white flag or something to show them we're friendly."

"We got a white shield here," one of the propmen said.

"That'll do, give it to Ottar."

The little boats slowed as they neared the beach, nine of them in all, with two or three men in each boat. They were wary, most of them gripping spears and short bows, but

[1] "Great Odin!"
[2] "Axes, swords!"

they did not look as though they were going to attack. Some of the Norse women came down to the beach to see what was happening and their presence seemed to reassure the men in the boats, because they came closer. Jens Lyn hurried up, lacing on his leather jacket.

"Talk to them," Barney said, "but stay behind Ottar so it looks like he's doing all the work."

The Cape Dorset came close, rocking up and down in the swell, and there was a good deal of loud shouting back and forth.

"Using up a lot of film on this," Gino said.

"Keep it going, we can cut out what we don't need. Move along the shore for a better angle when they come in. If they come in. We got to find something to attract them, something to trade with them."

"Guns and firewater," de Carlo said. "That's what they always trade to the Indians in the Westerns."

"No weapons! These jokers probably do well enough with what they got." He looked around for inspiration and saw a corner of the commissary trailer sticking out from behind Ottar's house, the largest of the sod buildings. "That's an idea," he said, and went over to it. Clyde Rawlston was leaning on it scribbling on a piece of paper.

"I thought you were doing additional dialogue with Charley?" Barney said.

"I find working on the script interferes with my poetry, so I went back to cooking."

"A dedicated artist. What do you have in this thing?"

"Coffee, tea, doughnuts, cheese sandwiches, the usual stuff."

"I don't see the redskins getting excited over that. Anything else?"

"Ice cream."

"That should do it. Dish it out into some of those Viking crockery pots and I'll send someone up for it. I'll bet those guys got a sweet tooth just like anyone else."

It did work. Slithey carried a gallon of vanilla down to the shore where some of the aborigines were standing in the surf by now, still too wary to come onto the beach, and ladled it into their hands after eating some herself. Either the ice cream, or Slithey's hormones, turned the

131

trick, because within a few minutes the skin boats were beached and the dark-haired strangers were mixing with the northmen. Barney stopped just outside of camera range and studied them.

"They look more like Eskimos than Indians," he said to himself. "But a few feathers and some war paint will fix that."

Though they had the flat faces and typical Asiatic features of the Eskimo, they were bigger men, erect and powerful-looking, almost as tall as the Vikings. Their clothing was made of stitched sealskin, thrown open now in the heat of the spring day to show their bronze skin. They talked rapidly among themselves in high-pitched voices, and now that they had landed safely they seemed to have forgotten their earlier fear and examined all the novelties with great interest. The *knorr* fascinated them the most; it was obviously a sailing vessel, but infinitely bigger than anything they had ever seen or imagined before. Barney caught Jens Lyn's eye and waved him over.

"How are you coming? Will they do some work for us?"

"Are you mad? I think—I'm not sure mind you—that I have mastered two words of their language. *Unn-nah* appears to mean yes, and *henne* signifies no."

"Keep working. We'll need all these guys and more for the Indian attack scenes."

There seemed to be a general mixing along the shore now, as some of the northmen investigated the bundles in the boats and the Dorset opened them to display their sealskins. The more curious of the newcomers had wandered in among the houses, peering closely at everything and talking excitedly to each other with their piping voices. One of them, still clutching a stone-headed spear, noticed Gino behind the camera and went over and looked into the lens in the front, providing a detailed close-up. He turned around quickly when he heard a bellow followed by shrill screams.

A cow had wandered across the boggy meadow that bordered the woods and the bull had followed her. Though small, the bull was a mean and surly beast, with a cast in one eye that gave it an even more evil appearance.

It was allowed to roam freely and had been chased from the movie encampment more than once. It shook its head and bellowed again.

"Ottar," Barney shouted. "Get that beast out of here before it upsets the Indians."

It hadn't upset the Cape Dorset—it had frightened them witless. They had never seen a roaring and snorting beast like this before and were rigid with fear. Ottar grabbed up a length of pole from the shore and ran, shouting, at the bull. It scraped at the ground with a hoof, lowered its head and charged Ottar. He stepped aside, called it a short and foul Old Norse name, then banged it across the flanks with the pole.

This did not have the desired effect. Instead of wheeling to get at its tormenter, the animal bellowed and charged toward the Cape Dorset, linking their dark and unfamiliar shapes with the present disturbance. The newcomers shrieked and ran.

The panic was catching and someone shouted that the *skraelling* were attacking and the northmen looked for their weapons. Two of the terrified Dorset were trapped in among the buldings and they ran to Ottar's house and tried to force their way in, but the door was bolted. Ottar rushed to defend his home and when one of the men turned, with his spear raised, Ottar brought the pole down on his head, cracking the pole in two and crushing the man's skull at the same time.

Within sixty seconds the scuffle was over. The bull, the cause of it all, had splashed through the brook and was calmly eating grass in the meadow on the other side. Driven by furiously wielded paddles the skin boats were heading toward the open sea, while many of the packs of sealskins had been left behind on the beach. One of the housecarls had an arrow through his hand. Two of the Cape Dorset, incluing the one Ottar had hit, were dead.

"*Madonna mia,*" Gino said, straightening up from behind the camera and wiping his forehead on his sleeve. "What tempers these people got. Worse than Siciliani."

"It is nothing but a stupid waste," Jens said. He was sitting on the ground holding his stomach with both hands. "They were all frightened, just like children, the emotions of children and the bodies of men. So they kill each other. The waste of it all."

"But it makes good film," Barney said. "And we're not here to interfere with the local customs. What happened to you—get kicked in the stomach during the stampede?"

"Not interfere with the local customs, very humorous. You disrupt these people's lives completely for your cinematic drivel, then you avoid the consequences of your actions . . ." He grimaced suddenly, with his teeth clamped tightly together. Barney looked down and gaped at the spreading red patch between Lyn's fingers.

"You've been hurt," he said, unbelievingly, then spun about. "Tex—the first-aid box, quick!"

"Why the concern about me? I saw you looking at that housecarl with the wounded hand—and that did not seem to bother you. The Norse were reputed to sew up their wounds with carpenter's thread after a battle. Why don't you get me some thread?"

"Take it easy, Jens, you've been hurt. We'll take care of you."

Tex ran up with the first-aid box and put it on the ground next to Jens, kneeling at the wounded man's side.

"What happened?" he asked in a quiet, surprisingly gentle voice.

"It was a spear," Jens said. "So quickly, I never realized. I was between the man and the boats. He was panicked. I raised my hands, tried to talk to him, then there was just this stab of pain and he was past and gone."

"Let me look at it. I've seen plenty before, bayonet wounds in New Guinea." His voice was professional and calm, and when he pulled at Jens' hands they loosened and came away; with a quick slash of his knife he cut open the bloodstained clothing.

"Not bad," he said, eyeing the red wound. "Nice clean puncture into the guts. Below the stomach and it doesn't look deep enough to have got at anything else. Hospital case. They'll sew up the holes, put in some abdominal drains and fill you full of antibiotics. Try and treat it in the field and you'll be dead of peritonitis in a couple of days."

"You are being damn frank," Lyn said, but he smiled.

"Always," Tex said, taking out a morphine Syrette and cracking it open. "A guy knows what's going on he don't complain about the treatment. Helps him, helps everyone else." He gave the injection with practiced swiftness.

"Are you sure the nurse cannot treat it here? I don't wish to return yet . . ."

"Full salary and bonus," Barney said cheeringly. "And a private room in the hospital—don't worry about a thing."

"It is not money I am concerned with, Mr. Hendrickson. Contrary to your beliefs, there are other things in the world beside a buck. It is what I am learning here that counts. One page of my notes is worth more than every reel of your celluloid monstrosity."

Barney smiled, trying to change the subject. "They don't make film out of celluloid any more, Doc. Safety film, can't burn."

Tex shook sulpha powder onto the wound and applied a pressure bandage.

"You must ask the doctor to come here," Lyn said, anxiously. "Have his opinion about my leaving. Once I go the film will be finished and I will never return here, never."

Almost eagerly, as if to remember everything, he looked around at the bay and the houses and the people. Tex caught Barney's eye, gave a quick, negative shake of the head, and jerked his thumb toward the company camp. "I'm going for the truck, and I'll pass the word to the Prof to warm up the platform. Someone ought to bandage that Viking's hand and give him a bottle of penicillin pills."

"Bring the nurse back with you," Barney said. "I'll stay here with Jens."

"Let me tell you what I have found out, just by chance," Jens said, laying his hand on Barney's arm. "I heard Ottar talking to one of his men about the compass repeater on the ship, and they pronounced it their own way, so that it sounded like usas-notra. It shocked me. There is a word in the Icelandic sagas, mentioned more than once, about a navigation instrument that has never been identified. It is called the *húsasnotra*. Do you understand? It is possible that the word 'compass repeater'

135

has entered the language as *húsasnotra*. If so, then the impact of our arrival in the eleventh century is greater than any of us imagined. All the possibilities of this must be studied. I cannot return now."

"That's interesting, what you say, Jens." Barney looked toward the camp but the truck wasn't in sight yet. "You ought to write that up, a scientific paper, that sort of thing."

"Fool! You have no idea what I am talking about. For you the vremeatron exists only as a device to be prostituted to make a trashy film—"

"Don't be so free with the insults," Barney said, trying not to lose his temper with the wounded man. "No one was rushing to help Hewett until we gave him the money. If it hadn't been for this picture you would still have your nose in the books at U.C.L.A. and wouldn't have a single one of the facts and figures that you think are so important. I don't run your job down—don't run down mine. I've heard this prostitution thing before, and it doesn't wash. Wars prostitute scientists, but all the big inventions seem to get made when there's a war to pay for them."

"Wars don't pay for basic research, and that is where the real developments are made."

"Begging your pardon, but wars keep the enemy and the bombs far enough away so that the basic researchers have the time and the freedom to do their research."

"A glib answer, but not a satisfactory one. No matter what you say, time travel is being used to produce a cheap picture, and any historical nuggets of truth will be found only by accident."

"Not quite right," Barney said, sighing inwardly as he finally heard the truck's engine. "We haven't interfered with your research, if anything we've helped it. You've had a pretty free hand. And in making this picture we have invested in the vremeatron so that it is now a working proposition. With the stuff you already have you should be able to talk any foundation into financing another time platform and letting you research to your heart's content."

"I'll do just that."

"But not for a while, yet." The truck braked to a stop

nearby. "We have the professor tied up exclusively for a couple of years, just until we get our investment back of course."

"Of course," Jens said bitterly, watching them unload a stretcher from the truck. "Profits first and culture be damned."

"That's the name of the game," Barney said, watching as the philologist was carefully slid into the truck. "You can't stop the world and get off, so you just have to learn to live on it."

15

"Better to die like men than live like cowards," Ottar bellowed. "For Odin and Frigg—follow me!" He held his shield before him as he threw the door open, and two arrows thudded into it. Shouting with rage, he spun his ax and charged out of the burning building. Slithey, waving a sword, followed him, as did Val de Carlo, blowing loudly on the *lurhorn,* then all of the others.

"Cut. Print that!" Barney shouted and dropped down into his safari chair. "That winds it up gang. Go get your lunch so they can pack up the kitchen."

The propmen were spraying foam onto the trough of burning oil and it stank abominably. All the lights except one went out and Gino had the camera open, taking out the film. Everything was under control. Barney waited until the rush was over, then went outside too. Ottar was sitting on an upended barrel, folding the arrows back into his shield.

"Watch this, arrows coming," he called out to Barney and held up the shield. The springs whipped the concealed arrows into position with a thunk-thunk.

"A wonderful invention," Barney said. "We've finished the shooting for now, Ottar, so I'm going to move the company ahead to next spring. Do you think you'll have the palisade completed by then?"

"Easy. You keep your bargain, Ottar keeps his. We can cut logs for wall easy with the steel saws and axes you leave. But you leave food for the winter so we can eat."

"I'll get the supplies first before we move the company. Is everything clear? Any questions?"

"Clear, clear," Ottar mumbled, concentrating on getting the arrows back inside the shield. Barney looked at him suspiciously.

"I'm sure you remember it all, but just for the record's sake let's run through it once more, quickly. We leave you the food, all the cereals and dried and canned stuff I can get from the studio commissary. That way you don't have to spend the summer and fall laying down food for the winter, so you can take the time to build some more shells of log buildings and a log wall around the camp. If what the Doc said is right you shouldn't be bothered by the Cape Dorset until the spring when the pack ice closes in near the shore here and the seals band together and raise pups on it. That's when the hunters come, they'll all be farther north now. And even if they bother you before then you should be okay behind the log wall."

"Kill them, cut them up."

"Try not to, will you please? Ninety percent of this film has been shot and I'd feel better if you didn't get yourself slaughtered before we finished it. We'll check up on you in February and March, then bring the company as soon as we know the redskins are close by. Give them some trade goods to pay them to launch an attack on the stockade, burn part of it down and that is that. Agreed?"

"And Jack Daniels whiskey."

"That's in your contract . . ."

A brassy moan drowned his words, rising and falling unevenly.

"Must you?" Barney asked Val de Carlo, who had the length of the *lurhorn* curled around his body, the nodulated flat plate of the opening over his shoulder, and was blowing on it.

"This is a wild horn," Val said. "Listen." He licked his lips and applied them to the mouthpiece, and, with much puffing and cheek reddening, produced a barely recognizable version of "The Music Goes 'Round and 'Round."

"Stick to acting," Barney said. "You have no future as a musician. You know, I keep thinking I've seen that kind of horn somewhere before, outside of a museum I mean."

"They've got it on every pack of Danish butter. It's a trade mark."

"Maybe that's where. It sounds like a sick tuba."

"Spiderman Spinneke would love it."

"He might at that," Barney squinted as an idea hit him, then snapped his fingers. "That's what I was thinking about, the Spiderman. He plays all kinds of weirdo instruments in that beat joint the Fungus Grotto. I heard him once, backed up with a brass section and a drum."

Val nodded. "I've been there. He's supposed to be the only jazz tuba player in captivity. It's the most terrible noise I ever heard."

"It's not that bad—and it might be just what we want. It gives me a thought."

Ottar thunked his arrows in and out and Barney leaned against the wall listening to the *lurhorn* until Dallas pulled up in the jeep.

"Ready to go," he reported. "All the commissary people are waiting and a couple of grips who volunteered because they wanted to see if Hollywood was still there."

"Enough to move the supplies?" Barney asked. "Everyone on the lot will have gone home by now."

"More than enough."

"Let's go."

One of the big trailer trucks had backed onto the platform and a dozen men were lounging around it. Professor Hewett had the door to the control cabin tied open and Barney looked in.

"Saturday afternoon, and cut it as close as you can."

"To the microsecond. We shall arrive precisely after the moment the platform left on the last trip."

It took an effort of will for Barney to realize that, despite all that had happened during the previous months, it was still Saturday afternoon in Hollywood, the same day on which they had begun the operation. The weekend

139

crowds were jamming up on the freeways, the supermarket parking lots were full, and at the top of Benedict Canyon Drive, behind his private golf course on the top floor of his mansion, L.M. Greenspan was suffering his phony heart attack. For a moment Barney considered telephoning him with a progress report, then decided not to. Only a few hours had passed for L.M. and he wouldn't be worrying yet. Best to let sleeping studio owners lie. Maybe he should ring up the hospital and see how Jens Lyn was doing, it had been weeks since—no it hadn't, just minutes here. He probably wasn't even at the hospital yet. Time travel took a lot of getting used to.

"It's a scorcher," one of the cooks said. "I shoulda brought my sunglasses."

The high sound-stage doors were rolled back, and when the time platform appeared all the men winced at the sudden onslaught of subtropical light. The northern Newfoundland sky was always a pale blue and the sun never burned down like this. Barney moved the men out of the way while the big diesel truck rumbled to life, then clanked down from the time platform. There was a holiday air about the occasion as they climbed into the truck and rolled through the empty studio streets.

At the commissary warehouse the holiday ended.

"I'm sorry, sir," the studio guard said, spinning his club on its thong. "But I've never seen you before, and even if I had I couldn't let you into this warehouse, no sir."

"This paper . . ."

"I've seen the paper, but I have my orders."

"Give me a war ax," one of the grips shouted. "I'll get that door open!"

"*Kill! Kill!*" another called out. They had been too long in the eleventh century and had picked up some of the Vikings' simple solutions to most problems.

"Don't come any closer!" the guard ordered, stepping away and dropping his hand toward his gun.

"All right you jokers, enough of that," Barney ordered. "Just sit quiet while I straighten this out. Where's your phone?" he asked the guard.

Barney took a chance that someone might be there and called the administration building first. He hit pay dirt.

Sam, L.M.'s personal accountant, was there, undoubtedly cooking the books in private.

"Sam," he said, "it's good to talk to you again, how've you been . . . What? . . . Sorry, I forgot. It's just been a couple of hours for you, natch, but it's been months for me . . . No, of course I haven't been drinking, I've been shooting the film . . . That's right, it's almost complete . . . Sam, no . . . don't get excited . . . This is no more a one-day picture than the script was a one-hour script. We've been working hard. Look, I'll explain it all later, but right now I want you to help me. I want you to talk to one of the studio guards, a real thick-headed job, must be a new man. Tell him to unlock the commissary warehouse so we can clean out all the dry cereals and canned stuff . . . No, we are not getting very hungry already, this is trade goods for the natives. Pay for the extras . . . Sam, what do you mean you have to think about it . . . if we can pay them off in Quaker Oats instead of greenbacks what possible difference can it make?"

It wasn't easy, it never was with Sam, but he was finally convinced. Sam—who hated to spend money even if it was only Quaker Oats—took his temper out on the guard, who emerged from the phone booth red-faced and angry.

By five-thirty the truck was loaded, and by a quarter to six it was back aboard the time platform. Barney checked to make sure that everyone was aboard, then poked his head into Hewett's control cubby.

"Take it away, Prof, but let me get clear first."

"Am I to understand that you are not returning with us?"

"Correct. I have a bit of business here. You can unload these people and the supplies, then come back to pick me up in a couple of hours, say about ten o'clock. If I'm not here I'll ring you on the warehouse phone over there and let you know what's happening."

Hewett was feeling waspish. "I seem to be running a specie of temporal taxi, and I am not quite certain that I enjoy it. My understanding was that we would go to the eleventh century to make your film, then return. Instead I seem to be operating a constant shuttle service . . ."

"Relax, Prof, we're coming down the home stretch. Do

you think I would lose a couple of hours like this if I wasn't sure of the production? We do one more time jump, finish the picture up and that is that. All over but the shouting."

Barney stood by the door and watched the platform vanish into the past. Back to the wilds of primitive Canada, chapped lips and cold rain. Let them. He was going to take a couple of hours off, get some business done at the same time, of course, but that wasn't going to stop him from enjoying himself as well. He couldn't really relax yet, not until the film was in the can, but the end was in sight and he had been driving himself for months. The first order of business was going to be a first-class, deluxe dinner at Chasen's, that much at least he owed himself. There was no point in getting to the Fungus Grotto before nine o'clock at the very earliest.

There was an unreality about being back in California, and in the twentieth century. Things seemed to move too fast, there were too many garish colors and the stink of exhaust fumes made his head ache. Rube! Dinner—with drinks before, brandy after and champagne in the middle—helped, and he was feeling no pain when the cab dropped him in front of the club at a little after nine. He even managed not to be offended by the bilious green doorway with the red skulls and crossbones on it.

"Beware," a sepulchral voice moaned when he pushed open the door. "Beware that all who enter the Fungus Grotto do so at their own risk. Beware . . ." The recorded voice cut off as he closed the door and felt his way down the ill-lit and black-velvet-lined stairwell. A curtain of glowing plastic bones was the last barrier before the inner sanctum of the club itself. He had been here before, so the novelty of the decor did not impress him. It had not impressed him the first time either, being just a cut above—or below—the ghost house at a carnival. Green lights flickered, rubber cobwebs hung in the corners and the chairs were shaped like giant toadstools. He had the room to himself.

"A Bloody Mary," he told the vampire-garbed waiter. "Is the Spiderman here yet?"

"I fink he's in 'a dressing room," the creature mumbled around its plastic fangs.

"Tell him I want to see him, Barney Hendrickson of Climactic."

Spiderman Spinneke arrived before the drink, a lean, black-garbed, scuttling figure with large dark glasses. "Long time no see, man," he said, letting his dank fingers flap against Barney's palm. "How'z the pix biz?" he sank into a chair.

"Keeping body and soul together. Tell me, Spider, is it true you scored a couple of films?"

"It is true I did the music for a ragged piece of class-X crap name of *Teen-age Beatniks' Hophead Rumble*, but I keep hoping people will forget about it. Why you ask? Can't be you're interested in the poor old Spiderman?"

"Might be, Spinneke, just might be. Do you think you could write the music for a picture and record it with your own group?"

"Anything's possible, Dad. But that takes time, we got commitments."

"Don't worry about the time, I'll fix it so you won't miss a single show. I thought you might have the right sound for a picture I'm doing, a stirring story of the Vikings. You've heard of them?"

"Cert. Hairy cats with axes, go around chopping people."

"That's roughly it. Primitive stuff, strong. They have a kind of brass horn and that gave me the idea. An all brass score complete with drums, hammering away with primitive savagery."

"Real cool."

"Think you can handle it?"

"A natural."

"Good. Here's a C as a down payment." Barney took five twenties from his billfold and dropped them onto the table. Spiderman's fingers oozed across the black cloth and absorbed them. "Let's grab your boys and go around to the studio now and I'll give you the scoop. You'll be back here inside an hour." Where else they would be during that hour of twentieth-century time Barney did not trouble to say.

"No can do. Doody and I just fake up until the rest come in around eleven. After that we're on until three. We can't split before then."

The Bloody Mary slid down smoothly and Barney looked at his watch and convinced himself there was no point in going away and coming back again, and 3 a.m. on Sunday morning would still be okay because they had until Monday to turn the film in. It was all going to work out. Spiderman slid back into the recesses of the club, and at ten Barney got on the phone and talked to Professor Hewett and arranged a new appointment for three, then went back to his table and relaxed, as much as he could relax with the hot tuba, brass section and amplified drums. The Bloody Marys helped.

At two o'clock he stirred himself and went out for a breath of air that wasn't solid with cigarette smoke and vibrating with wailing rhythms. He even managed to arrange for two cabs to come to the club just after three. Things were workng out very well.

It was close to four before they pulled up in front of the warehouse, and Professor Hewett was pacing up and down staring at his watch. "Very precise," he snapped.

"Not too bad, Prof old boy," Barney said, slapping him on the back, then turning to help pull the bass drum out of the cab. Then, in single file, they marched into the warehouse, with Doody on the trombone playing "Colonel Bogey."

"What's the raft?" Spiderman asked, bleary-eyed and tired.

"Transportation. Just climb aboard. We'll just be gone a few minutes from here, that I promise." Barney smiled slyly behind his hand as he said it.

"Enough already," Spiderman said, pulling the trombone away from Doody's fluttering lips. Doody kept playing for at least five seconds before he realized he wasn't making a sound. "Flying on pot," Spiderman exclaimed.

Hewett snorted as the funerally robed musicians climbed aboard the time platform, then went into the control cubicle to start the vremeatron.

"Is this the waiting room?" Doody asked, following him into the cramped quarters.

144

"Get out you oaf!" the professor snapped, and Doody mumbled something and tried to oblige. But as he turned, the slide extended from his trombone and swiped along the top row of exposed electronic tubes. Two of them popped and fizzled sparkily.

"Yow!" Doody said, and dropped the instrument. Its brass length fell across the exposed innards of the tubes and sparks jumped as the circuits shorted. All of the lights on the controls went out.

Barney was completely sober in less than a second. He pulled the musician out of the instrument room and herded him, and all the others, to the far end of the platform.

"How is it, Professor?" he asked softly when he came back, but there was no answer. He didn't ask again but only looked on as Hewett tore off inspection hatches and hurled the broken tubes out of the door.

He sent the musicians away after he received a grudging "yes" in answer to his question, when he asked if it would be at least a couple of hours before the vremeatron would be fixed.

By nine o'clock Sunday morning Professor Hewett admitted that the repairs would probably take most of the day, not including the time needed to find replacement tubes on a Sunday in Los Angeles. Barney, hollowly, said that, after all, they had plenty of time. After all the picture wasn't due until the following morning.

Late Sunday night Barney fell asleep for the first time, but he woke up with a start after only a few minutes and could not get back to sleep again.

At 5 A.M. on Monday morning the professor announced that the rewiring was complete and that he was going to sleep for an hour. After that he would leave and try to obtain the missing tubes.

145

At 9 A.M. Barney phoned and discovered that the representatives of the bank had arrived and were waiting for him. He gurgled and hung up.

At nine-thirty the phone rang, and when he picked it up the girl on the switchboard told him that the entire studio was being turned upside down trying to locate him, and that L.M. himself had personally talked to her and asked her if she knew where Mr. Hendrickson was. Barney hung up on her too.

At ten-thirty he knew it was hopeless. Hewett had not returned, nor had he phoned. And even if he arrived at that moment it was too late. The picture could not possibly be finished in time.

It was all over. He had tried, and he had failed. Walking over to L.M.'s office was like trodding the last mile—which it really was.

He hesitated outside L.M.'s door, considered suicide as an alternative, decided he did not have the guts, then pushed the door open.

16

"Don't go in there," a voice said, and a hand reached past Barney and pulled his away from the door, which sighed shut automatically in his face.

"What the hell do you think you're doing?" he shouted, anger bubbling over, spinning about to face the other man.

"Just preventing you from making a mistake, stupid," the other said, and grinned widely as Barney stumbled backward, with his jaw dropping and his eyes opening wide.

"A very nice take," the man said. "Maybe you should be acting in films, not directing them."

"You're . . . me . . ." Barney said weakly, looking at

himself wearing his best pair of whipcord slacks, his horsehide Air Force pilot's jacket and carrying a can of film under his arm.

"Very observant," the other Barney said, smiling wickedly. "Hold this a sec." He held out the can to Barney, then dug into his hip pocket to get out his wallet.

"What . . . ?" Barney said. "What . . . ?" looking at the label on the can, which read *Viking Columbus*—Reel One.

The other Barney took a folded scrap of paper out of his wallet and held it out to Barney—who noticed for the first time that his right hand was covered with a bulky, reddened bandage.

"What happened to my hand—your hand?" Barney asked, gazing in horror at the bandage while the can was snatched away from him and the piece of paper was thrust into his palm.

"Give that to the Prof," the duplicate Barney said, "and stop horsing around and finish the picture, will you?" He held L.M.'s office door open as a page came down the hall pushing a handcart loaded with a dozen cans of film. The page glanced back and forth at the two men, shrugged, and went in. The other Barney followed him and the door swung shut.

"The hand, what happened to the hand?" Barney said weakly to the closed door. He started to push it open, then shuddered and changed his mind. The scrap of paper caught his attention and he unfolded it. It was part of a sheet of ordinary writing paper, torn along one edge and blank on one side. There was no writing on the other side either, just a sketch that had been drawn quickly with a ball-point pen.

It meant nothing to Barney. He folded it and put it away in his wallet—and with a sudden jar he remembered the cans of film.

"I've finished the picture!" he cried aloud. "It's done and I've just delivered it on time." Two passing secretaries turned their heads and giggled at him; he scowled back at them and walked away.

What had the other Barney said to him? Stop horsing

147

around and finish the film. Would he finish it? It looked like he would—if there had been anything in the cans. But

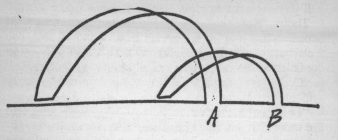

how could he finish it now, after the deadline, and still turn it in on time?

"I don't understand," he mumbled to himself as he walked across the lot to sound stage B. Even the sight of the professor working on the vremeatron did not disturb his whirling thoughts. He stood on the time platform and tried to understand what had happened, or what was going to happen, but fatigue combined with the shock of talking to himself had temporarily disconnected his reasoning powers.

"The repairs are finished," Professor Hewett said, wiping his hands on a rag. "We can return now to the year 1005."

"Take it away," Barney said, and reached for his wallet.

Even though it was a sunny day in Newfoundland it appeared dull after the California sunlight, and the air was certainly a good deal cooler.

"What time did we leave the studio just now?" Barney asked.

"1203 hours on Monday. And no complaints, if you please. That was very fast work I did on the repairs when you consider the damage done by that microcephalic musical oaf."

"No complaints, Prof. I'm beginning to think we still stand a chance to get this picture in by the deadline. I met myself in the building, and I saw myself delivering cans of film labeled *Viking Columbus*."

148

"Impossible!"

"Very easy to say, but maybe you have as big a shock coming as I had. I told me, or he told me or however the hell you say it, to give this to you. Can you figure it out?"

The professor took one glance at the paper and smiled broadly. "Of course," he said. "How stupid of me. The facts were obvious, right under my nose all the time, so to speak, and I never saw them. How simple the problem is."

"Could you bring yourself to explain it to me?" Barney said impatiently.

"The diagram represents two voyages through time, and the smaller arc on the right is the one that is of interest because it explains where the other 'you' came from with the cans of film. Yes, it is possible to still complete the film and deliver it before the specified deadline."

"How?" Barney asked, squinting at the diagram, which conveyed exactly nothing to him.

"You will now complete the picture, and it is of no importance how much time you consume after the deadline. When the picture is complete you will be at point B on this diagram. Point A is the time the film is due, and you simply return to a time before A, deliver the picture, then return to B. How magnificently simple."

Barney clutched the paper. "Let me get this straight. Are you telling me that I can make the film *after* the deadline, then return to a time before the deadline to deliver the film?"

"I am."

"It sounds nuts."

"Intelligence resembles insanity only to the stupid."

"I'll forget that remark—if you can answer me one thing. This piece of paper with the diagram"—he shook it under the professor's nose—"who drew it."

"I'm sure I do not know, having just seen it for the first time."

"Then think. I was handed this paper on Monday morning in front of L.M.'s office. I show it to you now. Then I'm going to put it in my wallet and carry it around until the picture is finished. Then I'll travel back in time to deliver the picture to L.M. I meet the old me in front of the office, take the diagram out of my wallet and hand it

149

over to myself to be put back into the wallet and so forth. Now does that make sense to you?"

"Yes. I see nothing to get disturbed about."

"You don't. If that is the way it is going to happen, then no one ever *drew* this diagram. It just travels around in this wallet and I hand it to myself. Explain that one," he added triumphantly.

"There is no need to, it explains itself. The piece of paper consists of a self-sufficient loop in time. No one ever drew it. It exists because it is, which is adequate explanation. If you wish to understand it I will give you an example. You know that all pieces of paper have two sides—but if you give one end of a strip of paper a 180-degree twist, then join the ends together, the paper becomes a Möbius strip that has only one side. It exists. Saying it doesn't cannot alter the fact. The same thing is true of your diagram, it exists."

"But—where did it come from?"

"If you must have a source, you may say that it came from the same place that the missing side of the Möbius strip has gone to."

Barney's thoughts tied themselves into a tight knot and the ends flapped loosely. He stared at the diagram until his eyes hurt. Someone *had* to have drawn it. And every piece of paper *had* to have two sides. . . . With slightly palsied fingers he put the diagram into his wallet, slid the wallet into his pocket and hoped that he would be able to forget about it.

"Ready for the time jump whenever you give the word," Dallas said.

"What time jump?" Barney asked, blinking at the stunt man, who was standing before him.

"The jump to next spring, 1006, that we were talking about half an hour ago. The food has been turned over to Ottar, and the company is all loaded up and ready to go when you say the word." He pointed to the waiting rows of trucks and trailers.

"To next spring, yes, you're right. Do you know what a paradox is, Dallas?"

"The Spanish barber who shaves every guy in town who

150

doesn't shave himself—so who shaves the barber?"

"That's the idea—only worse." Then Barney suddenly remembered the bandaged hand and he held up his right hand and examined it carefully on both sides. "What happened to my hand?"

"It looks great to me," Dallas said. "You want a drink?"

"It wouldn't help. I just met myself with a bloody, bandaged hand and I wouldn't even tell myself how it happened or how bad it was. Do you realize what that means?"

"Yeah. You need maybe two drinks."

"No matter what you and your Iron Age buddies think, alcohol is not the answer to all problems. It means that I am something unique in the universe. I am a sadomasochist. Everyone else, poor slobs, is limited to being masochistic to themselves or sadistic to others. But I can get a masochistic kick by being sadistic to myself. No other neurotic can make this statement." He shivered. "I think I can use that drink."

"I got it right here."

The drink turned out to be a bargain brand of cheap rve that tasted like formic acid, and it etched such a burning track down Barney's throat that it did take his mind off the paradoxes of time and his own sado-compensatory inclinations. "Go take a look, will you Dallas?" he said. "Jump forward to March and find out if any Indians have been sighted yet. If Ottar says no, keep moving forward, a week at a time, until they have been seen, then report back."

Barney stood clear while the time platform flickered and settled down a few feet from its original position. Dallas climbed down from it and walked over, rasping his palm across his black growth of beard.

"The Prof figures we were away about ten hours in all," Dallas said. "That will be overtime after eight—"

"Save it! What did you find out?"

"They got a wall put up, all logs like one of those forts in an Indian movie. Everything's quiet in the beginning of March, but on the last stop, the twenty-first, they spotted a couple of those skin boats."

151

"Good enough. Let's move. Tell the Prof to start shuttling the whole company through to the twenty-second. Is everything and everybody here?"

"Betty checked the invoices and she says okay to that part. Me and Tex called the roll and everyone's present and accounted for and in the trailers, except for the drivers that is."

"How's the March weather?"

"Sunny, but still with a nip in the air."

"Pass the word about that, to dress up warmly. I don't want the whole company down with colds."

Barney walked back to his trailer and found his overcoat and gloves. By the time he returned to the head of the convoy the shuttle was in operation. He rode through into the spring of the year 1006, and a good northern spring it was, too. Watery sunshine did not do much to take the chill out of the air, and there was snow in the hollows and against the north side of the log palisade in the valley below. It did look like a Western fort. Barney signaled to the driver of the pickup that had just arrived on the time platform.

"Take me down there, will you?" he said.

"Next stop Fort Apache," the driver told him.

Some of the northmen were beginning to straggle up the hill toward the arriving movie company, and the pickup drove past them and pulled up before a narrow opening where a loose log had been pulled aside to make an entrance into the stockade. Ottar was squeezing out through it when they arrived.

"We're going to have to cut a gate here," Barney told him. "A big double gate with a sliding bar inside to lock it."

"No good, too big, too easy to break through. This is the way to do it."

"You haven't been going to the right films . . ."

Barney's voice ran down into silence as Slithey squeezed through the opening behind Ottar. She was wearing a none too clean dress with a caribou-skin robe pinned over her shoulders. She didn't have on any makeup and she was carrying a baby on her hip.

"What are you doing here?" he asked querulously, feeling very put upon, that he had had more than enough shocks for one day.

"I been here awhile," she said, and put her finger into the baby's mouth and he sucked on it loudly.

"Look, we just came, what's with the kid?"

"It's funny, really," she said, and giggled to prove it. "After we were ready to go last summer, it was so long waiting in the trailer that I went out for a walk, fresh air, you know."

"I don't know, and I have a feeling I don't want to. Are you telling me that you spent the whole time here instead of making the jump with the rest of us?"

"That's just what happened, I was so surprised. I went for this walk and I met Ottar, and one thing led to another, you know . . ."

"This time I do know."

"And before I realized it everyone was gone. I was frightened, I tell you. I must have cried for weeks and weeks, and going accidental like that I didn't take my pills with me."

"That's yours then?" Barney said, pointing.

"Yes, isn't he sweet? We don't even have a name for him yet, but I call him Snorey, just like the dwarf in Snow White, because when he's asleep he snores all the time."

"There was no dwarf named Snorey," Barney said, and thought fast. "Look, Slithey, we can't go back and undo this now, not with the baby and everything, and it was your fault you left the trailer."

"Oh, I'm not blaming anyone," she said. "Once I got used to it it wasn't so bad, and Ottar kept telling me you would be here in the spring, and he was right. Only thing, I could use a real square meal, the way these people eat, gosh! I think I spent most of the winter on nothing but Whiskey and Wheaties."

"We'll have a big party tonight, for you and Ottar—and the baby. Steak and wine, the works."

Snorey began to howl and Slithey swung him around and began to open the top of her dress.

"I'll get Charley Chang working," Barney said. "We'll

write the kid into the script. This picture is going to be full of surprises."

This brought back a painful memory and he looked down at his right hand and wondered *how* and *when*, then jammed it deep into the safety of his pocket.

17

The stone-headed spear had gone right through the side of the motorboat and was stuck into the flooring.

"I left it there to plug the hole," Tex said. "A few more came close but we was already leaving."

"They must have been surprised or something," Barney said. "Maybe the sound of the motor frightened them."

"We were paddling."

"There had to have been a reason. The Cape Dorset are a peaceful people, you saw the way they behaved when they came here."

"Maybe they didn't like the idea of their relatives being chopped down when they acted friendly the first time," Dallas broke in. "We didn't go looking for trouble now, they gave it free without asking. If the motor hadn't started first pull we would have had a burial at sea or gone into their cooking pot or something. Tex and I talked it over on the way back, and we figured that we should get combat pay for this mission . . ."

"Make a note of it on your voucher, I'll see what can be done—but just don't bug me about it now." Barney pulled on the spear but it wouldn't come free. "I've got a few more important things to worry about. This picture is just about finished, except for the absolutely vital and very important Indian battle. We have to have it, and it is going to be a little difficult to have an Indian battle without Indians. There are a couple of thousand of them offshore there on the ice, and I send you out with the wampum and the beads to hire a couple and what do I get? Excuses."

The stunt men were unimpressed by this argument and

154

Dallas pointed coldly to the spear. A brassy wail split the air.

"Do they have to do that here?" Barney snapped.

"As I remember, it was your order," Tex told him. "The only place they wouldn't bother people with their playing was on the beach."

The black-robed procession filed down onto the shore, with the drummer beating time and Spiderman leading the way. They carried folding chairs, as well as their instruments, and were wrapped in an exotic collection of scarves, deerskins and caribou robes.

"Pull the boat up on the beach and let's get out of here," Barney said.

"I second that," Dallas grunted. "These rehearsal sessions are but murder."

Spiderman tottered across the sand toward them, clutching his tube to his chest, his red nose standing out starkly against the pallor of his skin.

"We gotta get a rehearsal hall, Barney," he pleaded. "All this fresh air will kill us for cert. Some of these cats haven't been outdoors in years."

"It'll clean their lungs out."

"They like 'em dirty."

"I'll see what I can arrange—"

"Enemy in sight!" Tex shouted. "Look at that task force."

It was an astonishing sight. From behind the islands that stood in the mouth of the bay came boatload after boatload of Cape Dorset, more and more until the water was dark with them. As they came closer a flickering could be seen in the air above each boat and a deep humming filled the air.

"This ain't no social call," Tex said.

"They might be friendly," Barney said with very little enthusiasm.

"How much you wanta bet?" Dallas said scornfully.

"All right—so we take, what do you call it, a defensive position. What do you suggest?"

Tex pointed his thumb at Dallas and said, "He has the seniority, so he issues the orders."

"Right then," Dallas snapped. "We get the civilians off

the beach, we pass the word to Ottar to lock up his fort, we pull back to the camp. We form the vehicles into a circle with the house trailers inside, and pass out weapons to all the guys who have seen service. Then we sit tight. Tex, start the civilians back to the camp."

"It sounds all right," Barney agreed. "But aren't you forgetting that we still have a movie to make? I want Gino and his camera on the hill there, overlooking the whole thing. And I should have another camera, hand held maybe, inside the stockade to film them when they come up." He ran through the possible second cameramen and arrived at the inevitable, though depressing, conclusion that he was the only qualified one available. "I guess I'll have to go in with Ottar and his crowd."

"If that's the way you want it," Dallas said, and watched thoughtfully for a moment while the musicians fled back the way they had come. "Gino and his camera go in the back of the truck. The truck will be on the hill and it will have a driver. Since the truck is between the beach and the camp, Tex can ride shotgun on it—and he's in charge. When he says pull back, they pull back. I'll come with you into the stockade."

"Good, it sounds good, let's go."

The forward movement of the boats slowed as more and more of them appeared, as though they were massing for an attack. Whatever the reason, it gave the people onshore time to set up their defenses. Once the movie people were organized to Dallas's satisfaction, he and Barney climbed into the six-by and bumped down the hill to the Viking camp. Dallas wore his pistol, had a submachine gun and bandoleers of ammunition slung over his shoulders, and unloaded some heavy and sinister metal boxes. They were the last ones inside the walls, and the big double gate, with the long wooden bar to lock it, was closed behind them. From the firing step Barney could see the truck back into position on the crest of the hill above.

"What makes the noise?" Ottar asked.

"I haven't the slightest idea," Barney told him. "Here they come!"

There was a ripple of motion that spread across the bay as the skin boats started in.

Barney rested the 35-mm camera against the top of the log stockade and panned across the line of advancing boats. Sunlight slashed down through an opening in the clouds and glinted from the spray and the chopping blades of the countless paddles. It was a grim, steady advance, and the blackness of the boats and the clothing of the men gave them the uniform of an army of darkness. The outlandish and frightening noise grew louder as the boats approached, and Barney clutched the camera and kept shooting, glad of the task that kept him busy. He had the feeling that if it hadn't been for that he would have turned tail and run.

"I've heard that noise before," Dallas said. "The same kind of humming whistle, only not so loud."

"Do you remember where?" Barney asked, zooming the lens in for a close-up of one of the leading boats. It was very close.

"Sure, Australia. They have these natives there, what they call Abos, and a witch doctor was spinning this stick around his head on the end of a piece of string so it made the noise."

"A bullroarer, of course. A lot of primitive tribes use them and they are supposed to have magical qualities. I'm beginning to see why, with a sound like that. There must be an Indian in each boat who is spinning one."

"I have magic here to fix their magic," Ottar said, whirling his ax over his head.

"Don't look for trouble," Barney said. "We have to avoid a fight if we can."

"What?" Ottar shouted, shocked to the bottom of his Viking spirit. "They want fight—we fight. No cowards here." He glared at Barney, daring him to answer.

"They're landing," Dallas said, stepping between the two men.

Any doubt about the peaceful nature of the visit had now vanished. As each boat landed the occupants dragged it up onto the shore and took out spears, bows, and soft quivers of stubby, stone-headed arrows. Barney concentrated on close-ups, Gino would be filming the entire action, and he could see the details of the weaponry in entirely too much detail.

"Ottar," Dallas said, "tell your people to get under cover and keep their heads down."

Ottar grumbled but issued the order. The Viking personality did not adjust easily to the concept of defense, but it was not completely suicidal. The defenders inside the walls were outnumbered at least twenty to one and even the combative northmen were forced to respect the odds. The first arrows hummed by and a spear thudded into the wood just below the camera. Barney dropped down and pushed the lens through a chink between two logs. It limited his field of vision—but was a good deal healthier.

"Coward weapons," Ottar muttered. "Cowards. No way to fight." He rattled his ax angrily against his shield. The Vikings scorned the use of the bow and arrow and believed only in the value of shock tactics and hand-to-hand fighting.

An impasse was reached when all the boats had unloaded and the Cape Dorset men surged around the log palisade looking for a way in. Some of them tried to climb the wall, but instant decapitation or dismemberment by the flashing Viking axes quickly halted this. The attackers waved their weapons and shrieked in their high-pitched voices, while the humming whistle of the bullroarers rose above all the other sounds. There was a small knot of men, to the rear of the others, that Dallas pointed out.

"Looks like the chiefs or whatever there. Dressed different, some kind of fur outfits with fox tails hanging off them."

"Medicine men, more likely," Barney said. "I wonder what they're up to?"

There was a concerted stir of action that appeared to be organized by the men in fur-fringed outfits. Under their direction some of the attackers were running to the nearby forest and returning laden with branches.

"Are they going to try and break the wall down?" Barney said.

"Worse than that, maybe," Dallas said. "These Dorsets, do they know anything about fire?"

"They must. Jens told me that fire pits and ashes were found in the ruins of their houses."

"That's what I was afraid of," Dallas said gloomily,

and pointed to the base of the wall where a mound of brushwood was being piled up.

All of the Viking spear poking and sword and ax waving was to no avail; the pile mounted higher. A minute later a man burst from the group of leaders in the rear, running through the shouting mob carrying a flaming torch. Viking spears rained down around him, but as soon as he was close enough he whirled the torch so it flared up and threw it in a high arc into the mound of brushwood. The dry wood crackled and flamed and smoke billowed out.

"I can put a stop to this whole thing right now," Dallas said, bending to open the steel boxes before him.

"No," Ottar said, putting out a restraining hand. "They want fight, we fight. We take care of that fire."

"Maybe—but you'll get butchered doing it."

"Butcher some too," Ottar said with a wicked grin as he started down from the wall. "And Barney wants good pictures of fighting Indians."

Barney hesitated, but it was impossible to ignore the meaning in Dallas's level, expressionless stare. "Sure I want a movie," he burst out. "But not at the expense of anyone's life. Let Dallas handle them."

"No," Ottar said, "we'll give you a good fight for your movie." He roared with laughter. "Do not look so sad, my *gamli vinr*,[1] we fight for ourself too. You will go soon and when we are alone we want these *skraelling* to remember what northmen are like in battle." Then he was gone.

"He's right," Dallas said. "But if he gets into trouble we oughta be ready to get him out." He opened the largest box and took out a weatherproof loudspeaker and a coil of insulated wire. "I'm going to put this up as far along the wall as the wire will reach."

"What is it?"

"The speaker for this curdler unit. Let's see how the natives act when they get a blast of this."

Ottar had massed all of his fighting men inside the gates, leaving just the women and the bigger children to man the walls. Two women stood ready to swing the gates

[1] Old friend.

open and, Barney saw with a shock, one of them was Slithey. He had thought her safe back in the camp. He shouted to her at the same moment Ottar raised his ax and his words were lost in the roar of Viking voices as the gates swung wide and the northmen rushed out.

This was the kind of fighting the Vikings did the best—and enjoyed the most. In a howling, compact mass they burst forth and crashed into the Cape Dorset. The superior numbers of the Dorset made no difference, for there was little or nothing they could do to fight these northern butchers, impregnable behind their shields and metal helms. Butchers is what they were, and their short swords and axes chopped and hewed through Dorset weapons and flesh.

The Cape Dorset broke and ran, they could do nothing else. They fled before the unstoppable advance of the blood-drenched killers. But, as the two groups separated, a space opened between them and the character of the battle changed. Swift spears plunged into the mob of Vikings, while arrows rattled against their shields. One man fell, with a spear through his leg, then another. The Cape Dorset began to realize what had happened and stayed clear, letting their weapons speak for them. The Vikings could not get to grips with the enemy—and close contact was the only way they could fight. In a few moments the tide would turn. They would be surrounded and picked off and killed, one by one.

"If you can do anything," Barney said, "now's the time, Dallas."

"Roger. I got the only set of ear plugs so if I was you I would put my fingers in my ears."

Barney started to answer him as Dallas threw the switch, and his voice and all the other sounds were instantly obliterated. As the wailing, sense-destroying thunder of the curdler exploded out there, there was nothing else he could do except jam his fingers into his ears and clutch at his head. Dallas nodded with satisfaction and dug smoke and tear-gas grenades out of the other box. With a professional, straight-armed pitch, he began lobbing them over the wall.

With his hands clamped tightly to his head, Barney

160

turned painfully and looked down. In those few seconds the scene had changed completely. The curdler and the bombs were as strange to the Vikings as to the attackers, but their reaction had been their natural one of drawing into an even tighter defensive knot. But not so with the Cape Dorset. They were overwhelmed by panic. The fearful noise tore at their ears. Pillars of choking smoke sprang up all around them and they could not breathe and they could not see. Without conscious thought or decision, they broke and ran for the boats. Where, a minute before, there had been an attacking army, there was now only a mob of fleeing, struggling figures and a scattering of motionless dark bodies on the ground. It was all over. The mob on the beach struggled for possession of the boats and a few last figures stumbled through the clouds of tear gas after them.

Ottar's men stood together, facing outward and ready to take on all enemies, human or supernatural. The ones who had been blinded by the tear gas were just as ready to fight as the others. Their courage was magnificent.

When Dallas switched off the curdler the silence seemed to beat in waves and Barney's ears were numb and still filled with that incredible and sense-destroying sound. He slowly let his arms fall and straightened up. The Cape Dorset were vanquished and fleeing, there was no doubt of that: the Viking warriors had lowered their shields as they realized this and were waving their weapons victoriously. Dallas's voice seemed to come from a great distance, through many layers of cotton batting, as he pointed toward the truck still stationed on the hill above.

"They never bothered the truck or the camp, so Gino must have been grinding away all the time." He looked down at the laughing northmen, who were tearing the burning wood away from the wall. "There's your Indian battle, so it looks like there's your film."

Barney turned away from the dead and wounded and began to climb shakily down.

18

"This is the sunset we been waiting for, Barney," Charley Chang said. "Look at those colors."

"Let's roll then," Barney said, glancing around at the film company on the hillside. "Are you ready, Gino?"

"Just about two minutes more," the cameraman said, peering through the viewfinder of the camera. "Just as soon as that line of clouds moves in front of the sun so I can shoot right into it."

"Okay, then." Barney turned to Ottar and Slithey, in their best Viking costumes, Ottar with a rubber scar and gray touches, which were hard to see, on the hair at his temples. "This is the last scene, the really last scene, and we've waited until now to get the color right. Everything else is in the can. It's going to run, one, two, three, but we're going to shoot it one, three and do two last to get you in silhouette against the sunset. Now in one I want you to walk up the hill, side by side, take it slow, and stop right there at the top where that line is scratched into the ground. You just stand there, looking out to sea, until I shout *now,* then Slithey you reach out and take Ottar by the arm. That's the end of the first scene. Then Ottar you put your arm around her waist and I want the two of you to hold it that way, while we dolly back for the closing scene of your figures small against the sunset. Got that?"

They both nodded.

"Ready," Gino called out.

"One sec more. When I shout cut you stay there on the hill so we can run the camera in and shoot number two, which is the talk. Is that clear?"

It went off well. Ottar was almost a professional by this time. At least he usually followed orders without arguing. They climbed the hill together and looked into the sunset. Boards had been laid over the grass to make a smooth track for the camera dolly to roll along, and the grips, goaded by Barney's shouted instructions, moved it slowly and smoothly away so the figures of the lovers could fade into the distance.

"Cut!" Barney shouted when the dolly reached the end of the track. "Principals—just hold it on the hill. Let's move now before the light goes."

There was a concerted and organized rush. While the camera was being trundled to the top of the hill the sound men were setting up their tape recorder and mikes. Slithey was frowning over her lines while the script girl read Ottar's aloud to him. The sky was a flaming red as the sun dropped toward the sea.

"Ready," Gino said.

"Camera," Barney called out, "and not a sound from anyone, not anyone. Action."

"Out there," Ottar said, pointing, "out there somewhere over the sea is our home. Do you still miss it, Gudrid?"

"For a long time I did, but not any more. We have fought and died for this land and it is ours now. Vinland . . . this new world, that is our home now."

"Cut. Good, print that. I guess that just about winds it up."

Everyone cheered then, and Slithey kissed Barney and Ottar crushed his hand well. It was a very exciting moment because the picture was just about finished in most particulars, and by the time the closing scenes were cut, scored and spliced the film would be complete. The party that evening promised to be a very big party indeed.

It was. Even the weather cooperated and, as long as the radiant heaters were left on, the end of the mess tent could be rolled up. They had turkey and champagne, four kinds of dessert and unlimited drink, and all of the company and most of the northmen and a few of their women were there. It swung.

"I don't want to go," Slithey wailed and dripped tears into her champagne. Barney patted her free hand and Ottar squeezed her thigh affectionately.

"You're not really going—or abandoning your baby," Barney explained for about the twentieth time. He marveled at his own patience, but everything was different tonight. "You know Kirsten will be a wet nurse if you

163

have to be away for a while, but there is no reason for you to be. And you have to admit that having a baby with you right in California, when you weren't even pregnant last week, would be hard to explain. Particularly during the publicity for the film. So all you do is wait until the film is released, by which time you will have decided just what you want to do about the baby. Remember, you aren't even married in California and they got a word for that king of thing. Then, soon as you decide, you come back here. The Prof has promised to bring you back no later than one minute after you left. What could be simpler?"

"It will be months and months," Slithey cried, and Barney started to explain for the twenty-first time when Charley Chang tapped him on the arm and handed him a fresh drink.

"I've been talking to the Prof about the nature of time," Charley said.

"I do not want to talk about the nature of time," Barney told him. "After the last couple of weeks I would like to forget about the whole thing."

It had been a trying time for a number of them. Over four days had passed in California—it was now Thursday afternoon on the vremeatron's time-of-arrival clock—and it had been a very busy four days indeed.

They had been shuttling back and forth to the lot very often to do some of the more technical cutting and dubbing in the labs there. Spiderman and his band had been recording the sound track in one of the studios. There had been much doubling back in time so the facilities could be used on an almost twenty-four-hour-a-day basis, and in many cases the same people had crossed in the same time. Barney had one memory of three Professor Hewetts talking animatedly together that he would just as well like to forget. He sipped his drink.

"No, really," Charley Chang insisted. "I know we're all going a little bugs from almost shaking hands with ourselves, but that's not what I mean. The thing is like why are we shooting the film here at this place in Labrador?"

"Because this is the spot that the Prof brought us to."

"Correct. And why did the Prof bring us here?"

"Because this is one of the places he and Jens searched for settlers," Barney said slowly. Tonight he had patience for everybody.

"Right again. Now did you ever stop to think why Jens wanted to search for settlers here? Tell him, will you, Proessor?"

Hewett put down his glass and touched his lips with his napkin. "We came here because of the excavations carried out in this area in the early 1960s by Helge Ingstad. Remains of nine buildings were found and carbon-14 dating of charcoal fragments on the sites placed them around 1000 A.D."

"Do you dig what that means?" Charley asked.

"Elucidate," Barney said abstractedly, humming along with the throbbing tones of "A-Viking We Will Go," the theme song of the picture, which Spiderman was playing softly in the background.

"It is now the year 1006," Charley said. "And there are nine buildings in the camp below, two of which were just shells to begin with, which we have burned to charcoal for the picture. So there is a Norse settlement here in Epaves Bay in the eleventh century because traces of it were found in the twentieth century. So you could say there is a circle in time with no beginning or end. We came here to leave traces to find here to lead us to come here to leave traces . . ."

"Enough," Barney said, raising his hand. "I've had this circle-in-time thing before. The next thing you'll be telling me is that all the old sagas are really true and that we're responsible, or that Ottar here is really Thorfinn Karlsefni, the guy who started the first settlement in Vinland."

"Sure," Ottar said. "That's me."

"What do you mean that's me?" Barney asked, blinking rapidly.

"Thorfinn Karlsefni, son of Thord Horsehead, son of Thorhild Rjupa, daughter of Thord Gellir . . ."

"Your name is Ottar."

"Sure. Ottar is the name people call me, short name. Real name is Thorfinn Karlsefni, son of Thord . . ."

"I remember some of the Karlsefni saga," Charley said.

"I researched it for the script. In the saga he was supposed to have come by way of Iceland and marry a girl by the name of . . . Gudrid."

"That's Slithey's name in the film," Barney choked out.

"Wait, that's not all," Charley said in a hollow voice. "I remember that Gudrid was supposed to have had a baby in Vinland, and they named him Snorri."

"Snorey," Barney said, and felt the hackles rise on the back of his neck. "One of the seven dwarfs from Snow White . . ."

"I don't see what everyone is so concerned about," Professor Hewett said. "We have known for some weeks now about these circles in time. What you are discussing now are the mere mechanical details of a single circle."

"But the significance, Professor, the significance," Barney said. "If this is true, then the only reason that the Vikings settled in Vinland is because we decided to make a motion picture showing how the Vikings settled in Vinland."

"It's as good a reason as any other," the Professor said calmly.

"It just takes a little getting used to, that's all," Barney muttered.

Everyone said afterward that it was a very memorable party and it lasted right through until dawn and very little work got done the next day. But the pressure was off and there was no need for the overwhelming majority of the company now. They filtered away a few at a time, some for a holiday on Old Catalina, though most of them wanted to go straight home. They left, waving their pay cards happily, and lights burned all night in the payroll department of Climactic Studios.

When the film was completed to Barney's satisfaction and a print had been made and was in the cans, there were only a handful of people left in the camp, and most of them were the drivers needed to move the company out.

"You're not going to smell fresh air like this again for a long time," Dallas said, looking down the hillside at the Viking settlement below.

"I'm going to miss more than that," Barney said. "I'm

just beginning to realize that all I have been thinking about is the film, and now that it's done, well, this all has been something a lot bigger than any of us realized at the time. You understand?"

"I dig. But you have to remember a lot of Joes only got to see Paris because the government sent them there to kill krauts. Things happen, that's all, things happen."

"I suppose you're right." Barney chewed at the palm of his hand. "But don't say it. Sounds too much like the Prof's circle in time."

"What's wrong with your hand?" Dallas asked.

"Looks like a splinter," Barney said.

"You oughta get the nurse to take it out before she locks up shop."

"You're probably right. Pass the word, we start moving out in ten minutes."

The nurse opened the trailer door a crack and peered out suspiciously. "I'm sorry, everything is locked up."

"I'm sorry too," Barney said, "unlock it. This is a medical emergency."

She sniffed at the scope of the emergency, but unlocked the instrument cabinet. "I can't reach it with the tweezers," she said, with what sounded not unlike a note of malice, "so I'll have to cut just a tiny bit with the scalpel."

The operation took only a minute and Barney's thoughts were on more pressing matters until she dabbed iodine on the tiny cut.

"Ouch," he said.

"Now that could not have hurt, Mr. Hendrickson, not a big man like you." She rummaged through another cabinet. "I'm sorry, but all the Band-Aids are gone, so I'll have to wrap a little gauze around that, just for the time being."

She had looped two turns of the bandage around his palm before he realized what was happening and burst out laughing.

"A splinter!" he said, and looked down and realized that he had put his best twill slacks on that morning, and was wearing his horsehide jacket. "I'll bet you have Mercurochrome here, in fact I'll guarantee it!"

167

"What a curious thing to say, of course I have."

"Then wrap this bandage on well, nice and big. I'll show him, that sadistic S.O.B."

"What? Who . . . ?"

"Me, that's who. I treated me like that and now I'm going to get even with myself. I thinks I can treat me like that!"

The nurse did not say anything else after that, and wrapped the bandage wide and bulky the way he asked, nor did she protest when he dumped so much Mercurochrome over it so that it dropped onto her clean floor. When Barney left, chuckling to himself, she locked the door behind him.

"You hurt?" Ottar asked.

"Not really," Barney said, and reached over so that this time Ottar crushed his left hand. "Take it easy and watch out for the Indians."

"Not afraid of them! We've cut plenty of hardwood, get a fortune in Iceland. You bring Gudrid back?"

"In a couple of minutes, your time, but what happens then is up to her. So long, Ottar."

"*Far heill,*[1] Barney. You make another movie and pay with Jack Daniels."

"I may do just that."

It was the last trip and everyone else was gone and the time platform sat in the middle of an acre of flattened grass and muddy wheel tracks. The cans of film were in the pickup, the only vehicle on the platform, and Dallas was at the wheel with a red-eyed and sodden Slithey sitting beside him.

"Take it away," Barney shouted to Professor Hewett, and he took one last lungful of fresh air.

Professor Hewett dropped the truck and the others off on Friday, and only Barney and the cans of film rode the loop in time back to the Monday morning of the same week.

"Leave me plenty of time, Prof," he said. "I have to get to L.M.'s office by ten-thirty."

When he arrived he phoned, then had to wait at the

[1] "Good-bye."

sound stage until the page arrived with the handcart. They loaded the film on and it was already twenty past ten.

"Bring this to L.M.'s office," Barney said. "I'll go on ahead with reel one."

Barney walked fast, and as he turned the last corner he saw a familiar, hang-dog figure plodding up the steps. He smiled wickedly and followed himself down the hall right up to L.M.'s door, and the figure in front never looked back. Barney waited until he had actually pushed the door open before reaching over his shoulder and pulling his hand away.

"Don't go in there," he said.

"What the hell do you think you're doing?" the earlier Barney shouted, then took one look at him and collapsed like a second-rate actor in a ninth-rate horror film, all shaking limbs and popping eyes.

"A very nice take," Barney said. "Maybe you should be acting in films, not directing them."

"You're . . . me . . ." The idiot figure burbled.

"Very observant," Barney said, then remembered the diagram. He would be glad to get rid of *that*. "Hold this a sec," he said, and shoved the can of film into the other's arms. He couldn't reach into his pocket with his gorily bandaged hand so he had to grope around with his left hand and dig his wallet out. The other Barney just held the can and mumbled to himself until Barney pulled it back and pushed the diagram into his hand.

"What happened to my hand—your hand?" the horrified other Barney asked.

I should tell you Barney thought to himself, then saw that the page was coming with the handcart and he opened the door for him.

"Give that to the Prof," Barney said as the page went past, then couldn't resist one last dig. "And stop horsing around and finish the picture, will you?"

He followed the page in and let the door swing behind him without a backward glance. He knew, without the slightest trace of doubt, that it would not open, and enjoyed the sensation of being positively *certain* of something for the first time in his life. This sureness carried him past Miss Zucker, who was standing and trying to tell him something about men from the bank; he brushed her aside and opened the inner door for the page. A very pale L.M. looked up at him and six gray-haired, frozen-faced men turned to see what the interruption was about.

"I'm very sorry to be late, gentlemen," Barney said with calm assurance. "But I'm sure that Mr. Greenspan has explained everything. We were out of the country and I have just arrived with the print of the film he has been telling you about. A multimillion dollar asset, gentlemen, that will usher in a new era of cinematic art and profit for this studio."

The cans of film rattled together as the page straightened up the handcart, and Sam, from the darkest corner of the room, uttered a small and almost inaudible sigh.

19

"You will excuse me if I don't rise," Jens Lyn said. "The doctor is very strict about rest in the afternoon."

"Sure," Barney said. "Forget it. Does it still give you trouble?"

Jens was lying on a lounge chair in the garden of his home, and looked a good deal thinner and paler than Barney remembered.

"Not really," Jens said. "It's just a matter of healing. I can get around fine, in fact I was at the opening last night. I am forced to admit that, in most ways, I rather enjoyed the film."

"You should be writing for the papers. One of the critics accused us of making a poor attempt at realism in the torn-shirt-and-dirt Russian style and failing miserably. He claims that the crowds are abviously good American extras and he even recognized the piece of the California coast where the scenes were shot."

"I can understand his feelings. Even though I was there when the filming was done I experienced very little sense of reality while watching it. I suppose that we are so used to the marvels of the film and the strange places that it all looks the same to us. But, this negative attitude of the critics, does that mean the film will not be a success?"

"Never! The critics always pan the big moneymakers. We've already got our costs back ten times over and it is still rolling in. The experiment was a noble success and we are having a meeting today to talk about the next film. I just wanted to come by and see you, and well—hope that you weren't feeling . . ."

"Anger? No, Barney, that's over. I should apologize for losing my temper like that. I see things in a totally different perspective now."

Barney smiled broadly. "That's the best news yet. I admit you had me bugged a good bit, Jens. I even brought a peace offering, though Dallas is the one who got it and asked me to bring it to you."

"My goodness," Jens said, opening the package and taking out the length of notch-edged, flattened wood. "What is it?"

"A bullroarer, Cape Dorset brand. They were spinning them when they attacked Ottar's camp."

"Of course, that's what it is." Jens took a thick book from the table near his head. "How very nice of you to think of me, and you must extend my thanks to Dallas when you see him. You know, a few of the people from the company have dropped in on me, and I've heard a good deal about everything that happened after I left. In fact I have been reading about it as well." He pointed to the book and Barney looked puzzled.

"These are the *Icelandic Sagas,* in the original Old Norse in which they were written. Of course most of them were just verbal history for about two hundred years, before they were transcribed, but it is amazing how accurate they can be. If I might read you a bit from the 'Thorfinn Karlsefni Saga' and 'The Greenlanders Story.' Here . . . 'At the end of this time a great multitude of *skraelling* was discovered coming from the south like a river of boats. . . . They had staves waving counter-sunwise and were all uttering loud cries.' The staves must have been the bullroarers such as this one."

"Do you mean that Ottar—Thorfinn—and everything that happened to him is in these sagas?"

"Everything. Of course parts are missing and it is a bit confused, but two hundred years of word of mouth is a long time. But his voyage, the building of the settlement, the attack of the *skraelling*—even the ice cream and the bull that frightened them on the first visit—it's all in here."

"Does it say what—finally happened to him?"

"Well it is obvious from the fact that the reports were recorded that he lived to return to Iceland or to pass on the story of his adventures to other Norse who came that way. There are different versions of his later life, but all agree on his prosperity and long and happy life."

"Good for Ottar, he deserves it. Did you know that Slithey went back to him?"

"The Gudrid of the sagas, of course. I read an item in the paper about it."

"Yes, it was obvious her press agent didn't write it. Something about retiring from films to be with the only man I love and the sweetest baby in the world, on his ranch, which, while the plumbing isn't very good, is very nice and friendly, with plenty of fresh air."

"That was it."

"Poor Slithey. I wonder if she has any idea where—or when—that ranch is?"

Jens smiled. "It doesn't really matter, does it?"

"You're right about that."

Jens took a Xerox copy from the back of the book. "I've been saving this for you, in case you came by. One of my students ran across it and thought it might amuse me. It's a copy of an item from the New York *Times,* 1935 I believe."

"Disturbance upsets meeting," Barney read. "Congress of the Archeological Society disrupted when two attendees scuffled in the anteroom. . . . Threats of suit for slander . . . claims that Dr. Perkins attempted a hoax by presenting the fragment of a glass bottle, claiming that he found it in a Norse middenheap in Newfoundland. Declared a fraud because this particular form has never been associated with any of the northern cultures, it appears to be too well made and in fact resembles the shape of container used by a well-known proprietary brand of American bourbon whiskey. . . ."

Barney smiled and handed the paper back. "Looks like Ottar has had some trouble getting rid of his empties." He rose. "I hate to run off like this, but I'm already late for the meeting."

"Just one more item before you go. In these sagas a name keeps cropping up, a man who seems to have had an influencing factor on the Vinland settlements. He appears in all the sagas, is supposed to have been on one or more voyages and even to have sold the boat to Thorfinn that he used to make his journey to Vinland."

"I know, that must be—what's his name—Thorvald Eriksson—the guy Ottar got his boat from."

"No that's not his name. It's Bjarni Herjolfsson."

"That's very interesting, Jens, but I really do have to run now."

Barney was out in the street before he realized what Barney Hendrickson might sound like after the Vikings had passed it on by word of mouth for two hundred years.

"They even wrote a part in for me!" he gasped.

"Go right in, Mr. Hendrickson," Miss Zucker said, and she even smiled slightly. She was the perfect barometer and Barney knew that his stock was soaring in Climactic.

"We were waiting for you," L.M. said when he came in. "Have a cigar."

Barney took it and put it into his breast pocket as he nodded around at the others.

"How do you like it?" L.M. asked, pointing to the stuffed tiger's head on the wall. "I got the rest home making a rug."

"Greatest," Barney said. "But I never saw a tiger like that before." The head was almost a yard long and two immense canine teeth, each twelve inches or more, protruded down below the lower jaw.

"It's a sword-tooth tiger," L.M. said proudly.

"Are you sure you don't mean saber-tooth?"

"So? A saber is a kind of sword, isn't it? Those two stunt men, what's their names? gave it to me. They are

173

running some kind of safaris, hunting, you know, and Climactic is getting a percentage of the gross for no investment at all except they use some of our equipment."

"Very nice," Barney said.

"Which is enough," L.M. said, rapping on the desk with his gold lighter. "I'm as sociable as the next guy, maybe better, but we have some work to do. We have to plan at once, immediately, to follow up the smash success of *Viking Columbus* with an even more smashing success and that is what we are here to decide about today. Just before you came in, Barney, Charley Chang commented that religious pictures are swinging up on the charts again."

"I wouldn't doubt it," Barney said, then sat bolt upright. "L.M., no . . ."

But L.M. was smiling and not listening. "And that," he said, "gives me an idea for the absolutely infinitive religious picture of all time, a theme that positively cannot miss!"